Chili

Queen

MI HISTORIA

by Guadalupe Pérez

a novel by Marian L. Martinello

WITHDRAWN

TCU

Library of Congress Cataloging-in-Publication Data

Martinello, Marian L., author.
 Chili queen : mi historIa by Guadalupe Perez : a novel / by Marian Martinello.
    pages cm
 ISBN 978-0-87565-613-7 (alk. paper)
1. Teenage girls--Texas--San Antonio--19th century--Fiction. 2. Family-
owned business enterprises--Texas--San Antonio--19th century--Fiction.
3. Restaurants--Texas--San Antonio--History--19th century--Fiction. 4.
Cooking, Mexican--Fiction. 5. Selling--Chili con carne--History--19th
century--Fiction. 6. San Antonio (Tex.)--History--19th century--Fiction.
I. Title.
 PS3613.A78634C48 2015
 813'.6--dc22
                              2014043513

TCU Press
TCU Box 298300
Fort Worth, Texas 76129
817.257.7822
www.prs.tcu.edu

To order books: 1.800.826.8911

Cover photo courtesy of the Witte Museum, San Antonio, Texas
Designed by Rebecca A. Allen

*Dedicated to San Antonio's Chili Queens,
in honor of their entrepreneurial legacy.*

List of Illustrations

Recipes

Acknowledgments

At every book signing for *The Search for a Chili Queen*, someone in the audience asked, "When is the novel coming out?"

My writing has typically been for teachers and young people. So, when I shared that question with my former editor at TCU Press, Susan Petty, she mentioned the Chaparral series of historical fiction for young adults. I had studied the people, their times, and their city when doing research for *The Search for a Chili Queen*. The age group felt right to me. And Lupe Pérez and her family and friends were alive in my imagination.

I am not a novelist, and writing historical fiction with all that it entails of plot development and authentic characterization turned out to be more challenging than I had thought. But I had the support and help of a wonderful team at TCU Press. And it is to every member of that team that I owe my gratitude.

The first reviewer of my initial attempt to produce a credible novel responded with a twenty-one page critique. I do not know the identity of that reviewer, but I will forever be grateful for the extraordinary insight and advice I found in most every line of that critique. After studying the review, I spent two years searching for ideas and ways to better tell my story. Then I rewrote the entire manuscript.

Interestingly, in these days of email and digital communications, I have not met any of the TCU Press team in person. But I feel their support and encouragement.

Dan Williams, Director of TCU Press, never waivered in his support of my efforts to write a good historical novel for young readers. He kept me going at times when I thought I might quit.

Kathy Walton, Editor, TCU Press, provided invaluable advice for improving the manuscript. Her careful reading and insightful comments on every line in every chapter caused me to see my characters and story more clearly.

Her review of Lupe's recipes helped me clarify them for contemporary beginning cooks without interfering with Lupe's late-nineteenth-century voice. Kathy's suggestions for rewriting significantly improved the work. I remain grateful for her thorough and sensitive editorial work on this project.

Melinda Esco, Production Manager, and Rebecca Allen, Marketing Coordinator, have also helped me to prepare my chili queen's story with its illustrations for publication and introduction to readers.

My long time friend and colleague at the University of Texas at San Antonio, Dr. Barbara Gonzalez-Pino, provided all English to Spanish translations and reviewed the Spanish-language words, phrases, and sentences used in this book. Barbara and her husband, Dr. Frank Pino, have been constant and ready references for all my questions about how Lupe, in particular, used her first language in this story's conversations.

The vintage photographs and maps used as illustrations in this novel are from the archives of the John Peace Library Special Collections Libraries of the University of Texas at San Antonio, including the Institute of Texas Cultures, the Daughters of the Republic of Texas Library at the Alamo, and the Witte Museum. I offer a special thank you to Julianna Barrera-Gomez, Melissa Gohike, Juli McLoone, and Tom Shelton of UTSA's Special Collections, Martha Utterback of the DRT Library, and Elizabeth Higgins at the Witte Museum for helping me find and share with you photographs and maps of places Lupe and her family visited, as they actually appeared in the latter part of the nineteenth century.

There is another person whom I must recognize. I first learned of her when Juli McLoone put me on to the manuscript cookbooks from the 1880s in UTSA's Special Collections. One handwritten Spanish language manuscript dated 1882 by its author gave me the idea for the signature dishes using chiles relleño, Lupe's breakthrough to success after so many failures. This story of Lupe and her quest would be quite different if not for that woman who recorded her recipes in her own hand, for all who would came after her.

Lupe and I offer our heartfelt thanks to all who helped bring her, her family, friends, and the various people she knew to life with understanding and authenticity. *¡Muchas gracias!*

CHAPTER 1

*I*t all began on the plaza that never slept—my favorite place in the whole of the city. In daytime, most people on San Antonio's *Plaza de Armas*, Military Plaza, were selling or shopping. After sundown, they came to have a good time.

From dusk to dawn, the plaza shimmered with the flickering light of dozens of kerosene lamps dotting the chili stands. I loved the aromas. Simmering chili. Stewing beans. Grilling corn tortillas. Steeping coffee. Flaming mesquite fires. And the sounds of chatter, neighing horses, barking dogs, cackling fowl, and crackling cook fires.

"*¡Vamos!* Let's go. Make yourself useful," Papá called.

Five o'clock. The plaza was in afternoon transition. Produce, wood, and hay vendors had dominated the scene since before first light peeked over the horizon. Now, they were leaving, and chili stands were setting up for the evening clientele. Chili vendors had plenty of competition. Getting a late start would not help.

Papá and my youngest brother, José, hustled to set up our stand. It was especially hard for Papá. When he walked, his body listed toward his shorter leg. All I knew was that he had suffered a serious injury when we were living at the King Ranch. Where I rode a pony. Played with dogs. Helped raise chickens. Went to school. Where I had many friends. Mamá said we should not ask questions about Papá's accident. As soon as he could get around on his own, we left Santa Getrudis for San Antonio. But

Papá was never whole again. The injury slowed him down a lot. Now he relied on José's energy and strength.

I was standing close to where Papá and José were placing wooden boards on trestles to form our U-shaped chili stand. We always set up behind San Fernando Cathedral and directly in front of Henry Wulff's tobacco store and saloon, the Kentucky Sample Room. Papá paid an occupation tax to the city to reserve our space.

"*¡Ayúdelo!* Help him," Papá said, nodding in José's direction. He and José had made several trips to get the benches, table boards, and trestles from the vacant room above Mr. Dullnig's grocery store on the north plaza.

José flapped a length of oilcloth over the tabletop. I caught the end. *Cotton tablecloths would be nicer than this*, I thought as I spread the slick covering over the wooden boards. Then I set down our tin-shaded kerosene lamps with their decorative cutouts, just like those that lighted all the other chili stands.

"Señorita, face this way, por favor," a familiar voice called. I turned toward the large camera on its spindly tripod. The hooded photographer snapped the shutter. I was in a photograph for the very first time in my life.

"May I see it, señor Hardesty?"

"After I develop the glass plate. When it's done, I will bring a print for you to see."

"Soon?"

"In a few days. When I am back on the plaza. I'll show you then."

"*¡Prestar atención, Lupita!* Pay attention! I thought you came to help. *¿Estás soñando despierto?* Are you daydreaming? Get the earthenware from the wagon and set the table."

I had asked Papá if I could go to the plaza with him and José well before the usual time, after dark. I had no idea that I would have my picture taken. Papá's reprimand embarrassed me. I *had* come to help. But that was not my only reason.

Yesterday, I overheard Mamá and Papá whispering about closing the stand. Papá said that it cost too much to operate, that our family would do better to send my sister and me out to do housecleaning and laundering. I was a halfhearted and careless housekeeper in our two-room adobe house with its dirt floor. How could I clean the huge stone houses in the King William area? I heard about their carpeted floors, expensive furnishings, and fine china. I knew I would not clean them well enough to satisfy their owners.

The plaza was where I belonged, where I wanted to be, among its people. Vendors selling produce, hay, or wood. Troubadours strumming their guitars to entertain. Stylishly dressed tourists gawking at the sights. Ranchers in fancy boots and well-shaped cowboy hats, doing business. City councilmen in bowlers and wing-collared white shirts, giving speeches. Gamblers in striped vests and string ties, making wagers. Actors and showgirls in fancy clothes, singing and dancing. Range cowboys looking for fun. Every night was like a carnival, a fiesta. How could I give all that up?

But Papá had reason for concern. Our chili stand was not doing well. Others had many more customers. Why not ours?

I waited at our stand while Papá and José urged old Caballo to pull our wagon back to the house to pick up my sister Josefa, Mamá, and the food. They returned as long shadows played across the plaza and another warm April day darkened and cooled. I helped Papá and José unload the large pot to warm over the wood fire they had laid on the ground at one end of the stand. Then Papá had to rest awhile. The heavy work wore him out. José built a second fire to heat the *comal*, the griddle that Mamâ used to make fresh tortillas, to simmer dark coffee, and to boil water for cinnamon-flavored, aromatic hot chocolate.

Our first diner arrived. I waited as Josefa served him and, when he was done, cleared his place. She handed me his plate, cup, and utensils. I mimicked the words she spoke every night while I washed dishes in the water barrel near the cook fire.

"Lupe, be careful to get them clean."

And every night, we had the same conversation.

"That should not take long. Not unless we have many more customers than usual."

Josefa was nineteen, two years older than me. And she was beautiful. She wore her long black hair pulled straight back from her oval face to reveal fine, symmetrical features.

On a wall in our house hung an old mirror that had suffered many assaults to its silver backing. The patchy image it reflected when I faced it was less than perfection. My face was too round, my nose too big, and my lips too full. But my eyes were large and glistening, like big, ripe, black grapes, Papá said. "They show the feelings of people in your stories."

I wanted more. To be honest, I was jealous of Josefa's good looks.

As the oldest daughter still at home, Josefa was our stand's hostess. I resented that, too. I wanted it for myself. And in wanting it, I knew I became more critical of her actions than was fair. Yet despite her beauty, Josefa was not attracting new customers.

Usually we had no more than five—and often not many more than that all night long. On the plaza's west side, the stands of Martha Garcia and Sadie Thornhill were always crowded, noisy, and lively. I wondered, *What are they doing that we are not?*

My chance to find out came this night. Josefa seemed content to keep the tabletop neat and clear of dishes. José and Papá had gone home to sleep. They would return early in the morning to take us home before going off to their day-labor jobs. With no customers ordering fresh tortillas, Mamá passed the time talking with some produce vendors who bartered fresh vegetables for a meal of chili, frijoles, tortillas, and coffee. I slipped away into the shadowy spaces and the crowds on the plaza, heading to where Sadie Thornhill was entertaining a small crowd. Sadie boldly proclaimed herself "The Chile Queen" on her *carte de visite*. It even had her picture. I imagined what mine might look like.

I counted thirty-three diners, some standing, waiting to grab a space on the benches around Sadie's stand as soon as one was vacated. Stylishly dressed men and women rubbed elbows with soldiers, cowboys, and tourists. Sadie dressed much like me, only Sadie's clothes were of better quality and not as worn. Her high-necked, long-sleeved bodice of deep blue linen lawn was nipped at her corseted waist and fitted over a skirt of the same fabric. The skirt's fullness was pulled to the back and draped over a soft bustle pad.

Sadie's porcelain skin glowed in the lamplight. Her bright blue eyes were animated in banter with her customers. Curls on her forehead bobbed as she laughed when one of the cowboys told how a rookie cook in his camp had a pot of dried apples swell up and overflow after he filled it with water. The customers vied for her attention, sometimes shouting over one another to be heard. A trail boss described how he hired a young, conscientious, and mannerly hand—one of the best he had known. He said, "When we got to a little town in Colorado, near the Colorado and Wyoming Railroad line, there was good grass for the cattle, so we bedded down for the night. After dinner, the kid told me that he wanted to quit. He was such a good hand, I hated to agree, but he was young and homesick."

Someone in the audience interrupted with "Would that have been near Hugo?"

The trail boss nodded and held up his hand. "I haven't finished." He went on to recount his conversation with the young hand. Then the story took a surprising turn that captivated the crowd at Sadie's stand. It was a good one for entertaining an audience at our chili stand, too.

"Would you hire me?" Sadie asked the trail boss.

"Sure would, Ma'am. I really like your chili."

This brought loud laughter and more curious passersby. More customers. Sadie's business was thriving.

A trumpet blared over the people's chatter. I turned toward the sound. Just as they did every show night before the performance, the Fashion Theater's brass band and entertainers spilled onto the plaza. Loud and rhythmic, the band acted like a giant magnet, drawing a crowd that formed a large semicircle around the performers. I ducked under and around the spectators to the front where I could see a dancer. He was quick footed and jaunty. His pinstriped suit fit him well, not like the frayed and baggy pants worn by the men in my family.

I joined in the cadenced clapping to the beat of his feet raising ground dust. He stopped suddenly in front of me, and I

Compliments of

Sadie Thornhill.

THE CHILE QUEEN.

SAN ANTONIO, TEXAS.

I learned a lot about being a chili queen by visiting Sadie Thornhill's chili stand. She had her own carte de visite, which she gave to customers. We used something like it to advertise our fonda.

Sadie Thornhill's carte de visite. Grandjean Collection. Accession number SC947. Por. S145. Courtesy of the Daughters of the Republic of Texas Library at the Alamo.

5

looked into bright blue eyes. He stretched out his arms. I reached out to grasp his hands. The next moment, my skirt was billowing behind me as he spun me around and around, faster and faster. Only my toes touched ground. My head was flung back, my hands held firmly in his strong grip. It was thrilling. Much too soon, he brought me back to the exact place where he had invited me to dance. Leaving me breathless, he gallantly kissed my hand and called out to the spectators. "If you want to see the rest, you will have to buy a ticket. Come on," he urged, "the show begins in half an hour, and we will keep you entertained until midnight."

No one moved.

"We want to see more," a man shouted. The redhead bowed and escorted a pretty blonde woman he introduced as Miss Rose Ward to the front of the band. She seemed to glitter in a brilliant red skirt and a low-cut bodice. A necklace with matching earrings sparkled in the flickering lantern lights. When she spread her arms, she seemed larger than life.

The crowd quieted, and Miss Ward began a ballad in a voice so small that we all went silent, straining to hear. Gradually, she increased volume. The ballad was one many in the audience knew. After the first verse and chorus, she beckoned us to sing along. A few did. She encouraged others. Before long, she had everyone joining in. After the last bar, the actress curtsied, responding to loud applause, then turned and walked back into the theater on the dancer's arm. Acrobats tumbled, and the showgirls strode after them as a barker called, "Four hours of entertainment for only ten cents, one thin dime."

The performers and brass band flowed back into the theater trailed by a sizeable, boisterous audience.

I watched, wishing that I could go with them. But I had no money. Besides, I had someone more important to see.

CHAPTER 2

artha's stand was crowded, raucous with cowboys, soldiers, and heavily muscled men. Their large hands were sun stained, roughened by work. Dotted among them were men of means in white shirts under suit jackets. And next to them were women in styles I had seen in the Butterick pattern book as well as in the Sears and Roebuck and the Bloomingdale's catalogs. Even from a distance, Martha's dark eyes flashed. I found a place close enough to take the full measure of this woman.

Like Sadie, Martha attracted a sizeable audience. Hers was a provocative presence. She wore a scoop-neck lace-trimmed chemise of white cotton with short sleeves. The lace hem of the chemise peeked out from under a bright red and green patterned petticoat. A green, waist-defining sash was knotted in back where its ends reached almost to her visibly bare ankles and feet in white satin pumps. The costume was striking and daring. I imagined myself dressed alike, then sobered at the thought of Papá's reaction to exposed skin.

The prettiest part of Martha's attire was her *rebozo*. The long silken rectangular shawl with a red and green woven pattern cascaded into intricately knotted fringes. It was much more than a garment. Martha flourished it like a matador's cape as she began her story:

"*Quatrocientos y uno*, 401 West Commerce Street—the Fatal Corner. That is where it happened, a little more than two years ago. Ben Thompson had dinner at my stand that fateful night—*sabes*, you know." She smiled and flicked the rebozo's fringes at one of the young men in her audience. I caught his nervous gulp and nod as if he were bearing witness to her assertion.

"*Sí*, he did. John King Fisher, too," she added for effect. "Ben, you know, used to be a lawman up in Austin. But here in San Antonio, he told me about losing all his money at a game in Jack Harris's Vaudeville Theater. He accused the dealer, Joe Foster, of cheating, gathered up his money and backed out the place, guns drawn. When Jack Harris learned what had happened, he let it be known that if Ben tried to come back, he'd kill him. But Ben did return. And when he did, Jack Harris was waiting with a shotgun. Ben drew his pistol and shot him twice, in his chest and shoulder. Jack bled to death. Ben claimed self-defense. After that, Ben quit being a marshal—because of the murder trial and all, even though he was found innocent. Took up professional gambling instead. To hear Ben tell, he was *uno de los mejores*, one of the best.'"

Martha shifted her rebozo over her shoulders, exposing her bare upper arms.

"*Esa noche*, that cool March night, Ben told me that he and King Fisher were planning to have a game or two at the Vaudeville, even though they had been warned to stay away by the new owners. 'Amigos,' I pleaded. 'It is healthier for you to stay here—with me.'"

I looked around at the faces of Martha's attentive audience. Just about everyone knew that Martha embellished the truth. But no one was about to contradict her. She told good stories—the best—because she had a vivid imagination and a flare for the dramatic. Even so, I had heard many versions of the Ben Thompson and King Fisher shooting. Who was to say which was right?

"'Don't you worry your pretty head about us, Martha,' Ben said, patting his holstered Colt and grinning widely as he tossed me a nice tip before leaving. I saved the coin." With her thumb and forefinger, she made a show of pulling a coin out of her sash and held it high for her audience to see before returning it to its hiding place. The crowd murmured.

"They got up to leave and I said, '*Ven a verme*. Come back to see me.' But I knew that was the last I would see of them."

"How'd ya know, Martha?" a tall man in white shirt and chaps called out from the rear of the crowd.

Martha smiled at him, patted her heart, and said to her audience. "I felt that something was not right."

"The way I heard it, Jack Harris's friends, especially Joe Foster, had it in for Ben," said a man in suit, white shirt with a black tie, and black cowboy

8

hat. He was seated on the bench on the stand's right.

With a quaver in her voice, she nodded and answered, "Not long after Ben gave me that tip—gunshots—from the direction of Main Plaza." She motioned toward the rear of San Fernando Church. "Beyond San Fernando. A big commotion! One of my regulars came running with the news. Ben and King had been shot. They said that inside the Vaudeville, Ben had offered his hand and a drink to Joe Foster. When Joe refused both, Ben got mad. He tried to be friendly, to let bygones be bygones. What would you do if a man refused to shake your hand? What would you do if a man refused to drink with you?"

A man to Martha's right raised a clenched fist.

"Sí. That would make you mad, too," she said. "So many different versions. The one I believe is this. They started to fight, Ben and Joe. One of Foster's guards, Jacobo Coy, stepped in, told them to settle their score outside. But Ben paid him no mind. He slapped Joe, pulled his Colt and cocked it, poking it in the dealer's face. Joe drew his pistol. But before Ben could shoot, Coy grabbed the cylinder of his Colt. Ben tried to get control of his gun. While he was scuffling with the guard, Joe Foster rushed him. King Fisher stepped forward to help Ben, but never had a chance to draw his weapon before suddenly, gunshots. And Ben and King were on the floor, their shirts stained red—*muerto*, dead. Both of them. They were murdered in cold blood."

"The inquest judged it self-defense," someone called out.

"*No puede ser.* It cannot be."

Martha waved her hand as if to brush away the comment. "How do you explain all the wounds in both men? Powder burns on both men's faces, Ben shot twice above his left eye and King shot right through his left eye. When they got Ben's body to Austin, two doctors," Martha held up two fingers for emphasis, "*dos* . . . said that there were nine bullet holes in him. They were .44-caliber. The weapon was a rifle. And they all came from above on the left. And—*pobrecito*—poor King Fisher. He took thirteen. Can you guess from where?"

The crowd almost chanted, "From above on the left."

Martha lifted both hands, palms up, as if to say *There you are*.

"Had to be Joe Foster's men who took their lives." Slowly, gracefully, she draped the rebozo over her head and signed herself. Then pressed the palms of her hands together, and with head bowed, murmured a prayer for the dead. We all fell silent, caught in the drama Martha had created.

A tall man in a well-cut suit broke the spell. "Never can tell what really happens in a gun fight, Martha. Now, roll me a cigarette, por favor."

Martha lifted the rebozo off her head and flung one end over her shoulder, making the fringes flutter.

"*Con mucho gusto, señor*. With pleasure," she replied.

I watched Martha press shredded black tobacco into a strip of cornhusk, then roll it into a firmly packed cylinder, twisting the ends. Holding it between index and middle finger, Martha raised the cigarette to the tall man's lips as he bent toward her to receive it. She struck a match and brought the tiny flame to the end of the cigarette. It glowed red as the man took a deep drag and appeared to savor the moment before exhaling a puff of smoke. He smiled, reached into his pocket, and dropped coins into Martha's hand.

I heard their clink.

Martha responded with a demure and quick curtsy. She had received more than payment for the cigarette. She had just gotten a tip.

My heart raced as I made my way back to our family stand.

"Josefa, *aqui no adivinas* . . . you will never guess . . . what I saw," I blurted out as soon as I saw my sister.

Josefa turned toward me, smiling, but she had not heard me. Her dark eyes were dancing.

"Oh, Lupe," she said, "I just met the handsomest man I have ever seen. He stopped by the stand tonight for a meal. He sat over there. Right over there." She motioned to a place at the table. "I asked him what he would like, and he smiled at me with twinkling blue eyes and said, 'Why, I would like some of your chili, señorita. I am told that yours is the finest sauce on the plaza.' When I served him, he did not wait for me to put the bowl before him. He reached up to take it, and his hand touched mine. His hand was smooth and soft, not like the calloused hands of a laborer. I asked him about his work, and he told me that he is an actor. He performs at the Fashion Theater."

"Did he have red hair?"

Josefa nodded.

"And was he wearing a pinstriped suit?"

"*¿Lo viste?* Did you see him?"

"*Eso creo*. I think so. With a brass band and some pretty chorus girls, an actor put on a little show in front of the Fashion Theater tonight. He even danced with me. What name did he give?"

Josefa's eyes widened. She raised her eyebrows. "Tom O'Malley. *¿Bailastas?* You danced with him?"

"Yes. A good-looking man, chiseled features, fair skin, red hair and blue eyes. I was standing with the onlookers when the band started to play. He stretched his arms out to me, taking my hands in his. Before I knew what

I was doing, he twirled me around and around until I was breathless and a little dizzy."

"Lupe, how lucky you are!"

"*Dime más.* Tell me more. What happened while he was here?"

"*Comía. Platicabamos.* He ate. We talked."

"*¿De qué hablan?* What about?"

"Well, he told me that he had just come from New York City. Imagine that."

"What else?"

"That he likes coming to San Antonio, because the audiences here clap and shout and stamp their feet when he performs. They greet him at the stage door afterwards. He talked about how nice the weather is here and how friendly everyone is. Then he said, 'And beautiful young women like you.'" Josefa blushed.

"You *are* beautiful, Josefa."

Josefa smiled. "I have never before been told that by so handsome a man."

"*¿Qué pasó?* What happened?"

"After he ate, he said that he had to get back to the theater, that it would soon be time for him to go on stage. He said he enjoyed the food and my company. After he paid for his meal, he dropped three pennies into the palm of my hand and gently pressed my fingers over the coins." Josefa reproduce the motion, smiling as she did so. "He said that he would be back." And she added in a whisper, "He said he wants to see me again."

"*¿Dijo cuándo?* Did he say when?"

Josefa shook her head. "*¿Para qué quieres saber?* Why do you want to know?"

"Just curious."

Josefa smiled, but not at me. She had a dreamy look. She was smiling at a memory. And then she returned to this moment. "Your turn, Lupe. What do you want to tell me?"

"I know their secret."

¿Quién? ¿Qué? Who? What?"

"Sadie Thornhill and Martha Garcia."

"The chili queens who get the lion's share of business every night?"

"I was watching them."

"And what did you see?"

"It was what I heard."

Josefa cocked her head and raised her eyebrows.

"Stories, Josefa. They tell good tales. Some are about real people and events. The stories are interesting, but it is the way they tell them that makes customers want to stay and listen. The better the story, the longer they stay. And the longer they stay, the more likely they are to buy a meal, then a drink. Maybe a second cup, then a smoke. The more likely they are to come back and bring their friends. We need to do what Sadie and Martha are doing. We need to entertain our customers, Josefa, with story-telling."

Josefa shook her head. "*No soy buena para eso.* I am not good at that, Lupe."

"*Puedes aprender.* You could learn."

"¿Cómo?"

"*Puedo enseñarte.* I can teach you."

"What makes you think that you can?"

"The family likes my stories."

"Family, Lupe, do not require talent. But customers? No, Lupe. I know that I have no acting ability. No one could teach me that, not even Tom O'Malley. And you? Be realistic. You have no experience performing for strangers."

"Josefa. Lupe," Mamá called. "*Es hora de cerrar.* Time to close. Your Papá will soon be here to take us home. Help me pack up. Hurry."

12

We had been working all night, with little to show for it. *We have just enough customers to keep the stand going,* I thought. *Martha makes more, a lot more. We can, too.*

Among the market vendors who arrived before sunrise were a few family friends who regularly ate breakfast at our stand. A small man— with a dark, deeply wrinkled face partially hidden by the wide brim of his hat—was wrapped in a worn and faded serape. He took a seat on the bench closest to where I stood. I knew him. He supplied our firewood.

"¡Hola, señor Gomez! *¿Cómo está?* How are you?"

"*Bien, gracias. Una taza de café, por favor.* Fine, thanks. A cup of coffee, please. Y tortillas y frijoles."

I poured the steaming dark liquid into an earthenware cup and placed it in front of the old man. He folded gnarled hands around the cup, as if wanting to warm them. Slowly, with the hint of a tremor, he brought the cup to his lips. He took a sip. The cup clattered against its saucer when he put it down. I brought him a serving of frijoles, mushy from overnight heating but still flavorful, with fresh tortillas Mamá had just made for him. His hands were steady enough to fold a tortilla, dip it into the beans and ladle them into his mouth. After a second cup of coffee, he rolled a cigarette and lit up, dragging deeply on the husk-wrapped, smoldering tobacco.

"How do you do that?"

"*¿Hacer qué?* Do what?"

"Roll a cigarette?"

Frijoles
PINTO BEANS

1 pound (about 3 cups) dried pinto beans*
4 cloves garlic, minced
1 onion, chopped
1 teaspoon cumin
½ cup chopped cilantro
1 teaspoon salt
Yield: Three cups frijoles

In a large pot, completely cover the beans with water (the water should rise about an inch over the top of the beans). Add the garlic, onion, cumin, cilantro, and salt to the beans and water. Cover and simmer for 5-6 hours, until beans are soft enough to mash easily, although you will not mash them. Check the pot often and add water as needed to prevent the beans from sticking and burning. They should remain immersed in liquid for the entire cooking time. The beans are ready when they are tender and fragrant, and the broth has cooked down until it's developed a rich color and flavor. Serve hot with tortillas.

We always served frijoles with chili and tortillas. Now and then, a customer might ask for only a bowl of frijoles and tortillas. We sold a serving for 5 cents.

*Canned pinto beans may be substituted to reduce cooking time. Add additional ingredients and use low heat until beans are thoroughly heated and seasonings are well absorbed.

His weathered face creased into a broad smile. "*Es fácil.* It is easy. Do you want to try?

Señor Gomez reached under his serape to a hidden pocket. He laid on the table a cornhusk and a pouch of tobacco. He tore a strip from the cornhusk and sprinkled tobacco shreds along its length. Just like Martha, he rolled it into a tight cylinder and twisted its ends, sealing the tobacco inside.

"Now, you make one." He guided me through the process of estimating the right amount of tobacco, packing it so there would be no air holes, and making a good seal.

"*¿Qué le estás enseñando?* What are you teaching her, Félix?" It was early morning but still dark when Papá arrived. He came to take us home before his workday began.

The wood vendor laughed. "This is a good thing for a young woman to know. A man will appreciate a wife who can make good smokes. For now, she can make some for your customers."

"Her mamá will not like that."

"*¿Por qué no?* It is good for business, no? You should teach your daughters to do these things. This one," he nodded toward me, "needs some practice, though."

Back at home, just before Papá left for work, I asked him about selling cigarettes at our stand.

"*Tal vez.* Maybe. I guess you could bring in a little more money. But you'll need to develop skill. I would not try to smoke the cigarette you made with Félix."

"*¿Y Mamá?* What about Mamá?"

"*Con el tiempo, se lo diré.* In time, I will tell her. First, you have an errand. Go to Mr. Kotula's grocery for coffee. While you are on the plaza, pick up a pouch of tobacco from Mr. Wulff. He knows what I buy. Just ask him for the same. Both merchants can charge my accounts." He flipped me a penny. "And buy yourself a candy."

I knotted that penny in the end of my handkerchief and buried it inside my rebozo. Then draped it over the trunk at the foot of the bed I shared with Josefa. I lay down for a nap in my chemise, covering myself in a faded Saltillo blanket with threadbare spots. Like an old woman, its once-vibrant colors had been dulled by the many years that have passed since it was born on a loom. But it still gave warmth and protection.

My nap was short, only a few hours, but my sleep had been sound. I awakened before the others and dressed hurriedly. When I pulled my rebozo from atop the trunk, the penny-weighted handkerchief fell to the earthen floor. I yanked it up by its loose end, tucked it into a small pouch I made in the end of the rebozo, and headed for the plaza. It was early afternoon.

From our house on Laredo Street, I walked north, turned right on Dolorosa, and crossed San Pedro Creek where women were doing their laundry. I continued on Dolorosa until I arrived at Kotula's grocery store on the south side of Plaza de Armas.

I first met Peter Meyer in Mr. Kotula's grocery store. He walked toward me down that long aisle between shelves, barrels, and boxes full of bagged, canned, and bulk foods.
Interior of Ed Kotula's grocery store on the south side of Military Plaza, General Photograph Collection, 1002: 073-1198, University of Texas at San Antonio Libraries Special Collections from the Institute of Texan Cultures.

A bell jingled as I entered the store. Its long, narrow aisle was lined from floor to ceiling with shelves full of canned, boxed, and bottled goods. Sacks of flour and sugar sat on a high ledge. Wrapped smoked hams hung from cord looped around a two-by-four that ran the length of the top shelves. A counter on one side held a scale to weigh goods sold by the pound, like the rice and dried beans in large barrels. Glass cases at one end of the counter held fresh-baked breads and pies.

A young man I did not recognize strode toward me. His long legs covered the store's length in loose, rangy strides. He seemed very tall and slender. The white shirt under his jacket was neatly pressed, its wing collar stiffly starched.

"Good day, señorita."

I looked into bright blue eyes the color of a Texas summer sky.

"My father is Jorge Pérez," I answered. "We have a chili stand on the plaza. I have come for two pounds of coffee. Please charge the cost to my father's account." I addressed him in my most formal English but was not surprised when he responded in Spanish. Most of the people I knew in San Antonio spoke a mixture of Spanish and English every day, with some

German, too.

"*Claro que sí. Estaremos encantados de hacerlo, señorita Pérez.* I am happy to do that, Miss Pérez. If you have other errands today, I can hold the beans for you."

"Thank you, but I must roast them this afternoon."

I watched as he scooped green coffee beans from a burlap sack into the scale's pan. "These are well formed. They will roast evenly."

His hair, the color of newly baled hay, was held in place with pomade. His complexion was cream colored, brightened by a little color in his cheeks. His nose was angular, his lips thin. He moved smoothly, with confidence, as he poured the measured beans from the scale into a small cloth sack and tied its open end with twine. A large, strong hand put the package into my outstretched one.

"Is there anything else?"

"*No hay nada ahora, gracias.* Thank you, nothing else for now. But perhaps you would like to have a plate of chili at our stand one night?"

"*Tal vez.* Perhaps," he answered.

"I am called Lupe."

"My name is Peter Meyer."

"*Mucho gusto.* Pleased to meet you. I do not remember seeing you on the plaza. Do you come at night when the chili stands are serving?"

He shook his head. "I have just arrived here. They say that there is business opportunity in San Antonio. I came to see for myself."

"Well, if you want to know San Antonio, you must see the plaza by night. Come by my family's stand one evening. Our place is in front of the Kentucky Sample Room."

He nodded. "*Bueno.* Okay."

"And bring your friends."

I left Mr. Kotula's store feeling pleased with myself for promoting business. On the plaza, I skirted produce wagons, exchanging greetings with vendors as I passed. I headed east toward the rear of San Fernando and bounded into Henry Wulff's tobacco shop next door to the church.

"Well hello, Lupe," Henry Wulff said. "How is business?"

"Good. Very good," I lied. "But it would be better if you sent some of your customers our way."

"I'm not so sure you want them after they have spent most of their money on hard liquor."

"Our meals are inexpensive. Tell them they can get a good one for ten cents."

"Are you here to buy something?"

"A pouch of tobacco. What my father buys."

Mr. Wulff brought out a pouch from behind the counter. "On your father's account?"

I nodded. When I adjusted my rebozo to cradle the small pouch of tobacco and the coffee beans, I felt the cloth-wrapped coin.

"Now remember, Mr. Wulff, tell your customers to save a dime for a nice meal, only steps from your saloon, por favor. But if they only have five cents, we make a nice plate of enchiladas in our distinctive chile sauce."

He nodded and waved.

From the front door of Wulff's store, I looked past the place reserved for our stand. I scanned the plaza for a candy man. *El dulcero* was sitting on a crate near a hay wagon directly across from where I stood. A large tray hung from a strap strung over his shoulders.

He was a small man with a long nose and a thick, dark mustache and beard. His hat's floppy brim shaded close-set, kindly eyes. He flipped his paper swatter, though there were no flies buzzing over the candies, which lay on an enormous tray fashioned out of lengths of plywood and lined with paper. He was wearing a frock coat, buttoned at the neck, over a dingy white shirt with a frayed collar.

Elena's father, señor Hernández, made candies and sold them on Military Plaza. He became the candy man for customers at our stand.

El Dulcero, the candy man, with his tray of candy, San Antonio, Texas. General Photograph Collection, MS 362: 085-0069, University of Texas at San Antonio Library Special Collections from the Institute of Texan Cultures.

"Hola, señor Hernández."

"Hola, Lupe. You have the pick of my candies. You are my first customer today."

The twists of sticky *melchocha*, toffee, were pretty to look at, but my appetite drew me to the golden rounds laden with pecans. "*Una pipitoria, por favor.*"

"*¿Su favorito?*"

"*Me encantan las nueces.* I love pecans."

El dulcero smiled. "*Está bien.* That is good. We have many pecan trees here. *¿Cuál?* Which one?"

I pointed to a praline with lots of pecans sticking out on top. Señor Hernández wrapped the candy in brown paper and exchanged it for my penny.

"*Espero que lo disfrute.* I hope you enjoy it," he said.

I took a bite of the candy. The sweet taste of *piloncillo*, a type of brown sugar, and woodsy pecan filled my mouth. And then a thought occurred to me.

"*Tengo una pregunta.* I have a question. If my family asked you to, would you sell your candies at our chili stand?"

"Depende." El dulcero was cautious. "I sell here in the daytime, mostly to children. I do pretty well. I do not know if I would do as well selling to adults." His eyes narrowed. "I guess you would want some of my profit. So I would have to do a lot better than I do on my own."

"*No, no pensé eso.* No, I did not think that. I only . . . well . . . your candies could be desserts for some who take our meals."

"*No sé.* I do not know if I can change my ways . . . stay up all night."

"*Tengo una idea.* I have an idea. I just need to know if you would be willing."

"Only if I could do better—a lot better—than I do now."

"How much better?"

"Come back when you have a serious offer and I will let you know if I am interested."

Pipitorias con Nueces
PECAN PRALINES

1 cup ground piloncillo grains or light brown sugar
1 cup white sugar
3 tablespoons light corn syrup
1 teaspoon vanilla extract (Señor Hernández made vanilla extract by adding
    a cup of brandy to 5 whole dried vanilla beans and letting the beans sit
    for 8-10 weeks.)
1½ tablespoons softened butter
⅓ cup milk
2 cups pecan halves
Yield: 24 pralines

Place sugars and corn syrup and about 4 or 5 tablespoons of water in a well-greased medium-size pot.* Heat to dissolve sugars and corn syrup in water. Blend together with the vanilla extract, butter, and milk. Add the pecans. Heat just to boiling, stirring constantly so mixture does not burn. Reduce heat. Continue cooking and stirring for a few minutes, just long enough for a drizzle of the mixture dropped into cool water in a small bowl (one that is wide enough for you to reach into) forms a soft ball that flattens when pressed between your fingers. This will happen quickly so you must work fast. Be careful not to overcook or the ingredients will clump. When the candy ball flattens in water and is still pliable, it has reached the right temperature.** Immediately remove the pot from the heat and stir just until the mixture loses its gloss and becomes opaque. Work quickly while the mixture is still hot, as it will harden when it cools. Drop one spoonful at a time onto a well-greased flat pan.*** Most pralines are about 2 ½ to 3 inches in diameter. The pralines will harden into golden crispy candies. When completely cooled, remove the pralines from the greased pan with a spatula. Store in an airtight container. To prepare the pot for cleaning, pour very hot water into the pot and over utensils and let them sit long enough to dissolve the hardened sugar residue. Then clean as you usually do.

*A two-quart saucepan is about the right size.
**A candy thermometer will register 238°F at this stage.
***Nonstick aluminum foil or aluminum foil that has been sprayed with a nonstick cooking spray may be substituted for a greased flat pan.

CHAPTER 4

I practiced making cigarettes until I got faster and better at it. Papá inspected each one, feeling its length and judging its quality. He selected five.

"Bueno. I think these are good enough to sell, Lupita." He rummaged around in his toolbox and pulled out a tin that had once contained chocolate. "They will keep their shape in this. See how nice they look lined up in a straight row. The tin is airtight, but you do not want to make too many at once. They will get stale. While you are learning, it will be easier for you to have some already made. Later, when you are more skilled, you can make them fresh for your customers."

That night, humid air diffused the lantern light, rubbing off the sharp edges on everyone and everything on the plaza. At first I did not recognize the man who approached our stand.

"¡Hola señorita Pérez!" He removed his bowler and I saw his fair hair even in the dim light of the kerosene lamps.

I had not expected to see Peter Meyer at the stand so soon, but I was determined to be bold, "Well, Mr. Meyer. What took you so long?"

That ruffled him, "Ah . . . well . . ."

I laughed. "Please, be seated. What can I get for you?"

He hesitated.

"You would like my mother's enchiladas. They are the very best in San Antonio . . . maybe even in all of South Texas. My mother will make your tortillas while you wait. Our chile sauce has a flavor you cannot find anywhere else. I helped to make it."

"Yes, some enchiladas."

I sang the order to Mamá for effect. I surprised myself as much as Josefa, who was miffed. I had ventured into her territory. *But,* I reasoned, *Josefa may be hostess but no one can—or should—prevent me from talking with anyone I want to.* I turned back to Peter Meyer.

"When I met you in Mr. Kotula's store, you said that you had recently arrived here."

"Yes, I came here only a few weeks ago."

"From where?"

"Stonewall, in the hill country."

"You have family there?"

He nodded. "We have a farm. Cotton is our cash crop."

"You do not like farming?"

He scrunched his lips and frowned. "Not me. I come from a large family. My brother wants to farm. I want to try my hand at something different. My father's friend knows Mr. Kotula's family, so I was hired to work in his store. One day, I will have a general store of my own."

"A nice dream."

He nodded. "I can do it. I know I can." But his voice sounded a note of uncertainty, and I regretted that for him.

Mamá called to Josefa. The corn tortillas she had dipped in chile sauce and rolled into cylinders were ready. I watched as Mamá handed Josefa the plate, then ladled a little more sauce over the three tortillas, sprinkling them with chopped raw onion and crumbled *queso fresco,* fresh cheese. Josefa carried the plate to Peter, carefully set it in front of him, and provided a fork and napkin. I was jealous. I wanted to serve Peter on my own.

"We have café," I suggested.

He nodded. "Yes, thank you."

Josefa poured him a cup of coffee, steam swirling up from the cup.

He took a bite of the enchilada soaked in chile sauce and held it in his mouth for a long moment. I waited, wondering if he would like the Mexican spices. He nodded his head appreciatively. "This is delicious."

"Best chile sauce in South Texas. Not too hot. Our sauce is different that way. We aim for flavor, not heat. You should feel your tongue tingle and a sting in your throat, but it should not set your mouth on fire."

He smiled and continued to eat in silence.

I studied him. He seemed a quiet man, very different from my boisterous and fun-loving brothers and friends like Antonio Ortiz. *If I can bring*

22

Café
COFFEE

For each cup:
1 heaping teaspoon ground coffee (You will want to try different
    amounts of coffee until you find the right amount for the brew
    to suit your taste. We made strong coffee.)
1 cup water*
For every five servings:
1 cinnamon stick or ¼ teaspoon ground cinnamon
crushed egg shells

Put the coffee grounds and cinnamon stick into a coffee pot. Add
the water. Place over medium heat. Bring to a boil, then reduce heat
to a simmer. As soon as the liquid slows to a simmer, remove the pot
from the heat. Add a pinch of crushed eggshells to a quarter cup
of cold water and add to the pot. Let the pot sit for a few minutes
to settle the coffee grounds. Do not stir or move it during this time.
Carefully pour the brew into cups without disturbing the grounds.

Serve black or with sugar or honey to taste. Most of our customers
drank their coffee black. A few liked to sweeten it with ground piloncillo. Others preferred *azúcar blanco*, white sugar.

A cup of coffee is about 6 fluid ounces.

this one out of his shell, I thought, *others—the playful, rowdy ones—will be easy.*

Here's my chance, I thought. I began slowly, with a story I had overheard at Martha's stand. "Did you know that two prisoners held in the Old Bat Cave over there tried to escape?" I waved my hand in the direction of a building on the plaza's northwest corner that housed the jail, city hall, and the county courthouse.

Peter Meyer looked up quizzically. Josefa shot me a disapproving glance but said nothing to discourage me. She, too, saw Peter Meyer's interest.

"One especially dark night, they began digging a hole through the wall of their cell."

I read the question in his eyes and nodded. "Rock by rock. They chipped away at the mortar and removed each big stone."

Again, I anticipated his thoughts. "With bare hands? I do not think so. Probably with an iron rod."

"Now, how did they get an iron rod in jail?" He laughed.

"No sé. Someone must have sneaked it to them. Maybe a visitor?"

"And nobody saw or heard them digging out a hole in the wall?"

"They must have taken turns, one digging while the other stood watch. That is what I would do."

He sipped his coffee, seeming to ponder that thought. For added drama, I lowered my voice almost to a whisper.

"Once the hole was big enough to let them pass—it didn't have to be very big since they were wiry, like young cowhands—one after the other, they eased out from the cell into the hall, only to find another wall."

"They made another hole? How long did it take them to do all this with no one noticing?"

"*Oh, ellos fueron inteligentes.* They were clever."

I was now aware of two men who had just seated themselves on the bench near where I stood. I thought they might be drawn by the story, so I raised my voice.

"One stayed in the cell while the other worked on the outside wall. They kept all the rocks handy so that they could plug the holes when the sheriff's deputy walked by or brought them meals. When the holes were ready, so were they."

"They had to scale a fifteen-foot wall at least two feet thick," one of the newcomers chimed in.

"Ah. Sí, the top of that wall was studded with sharp glass when it was built. Shards from bottles, mirrors, and windowpanes were embedded in the plaster. But did that stop them?" I shook my head. "They got over that, and using foot and hand holes in the northeast corner of the wall, they scaled it."

"Did they get away?" Peter asked.

"What do you think?"

Posing the question gave me time to remove Peter's empty plate. Josefa took orders from the two men now engrossed in my story. "Would you like some enchiladas? Or chili?" she asked.

"A bowl of chili," one said, "for each of us, and some frijoles."

"And tortillas," the other added.

Josefa called their orders to Mamá. My sister was clearly annoyed with me, but I paid her no mind.

"How far could they go?" Peter Meyer's interest in the story was piqued.

"Far enough."

I lowered my voice to suggest secrecy, making sure that all three men could hear me. I did not know the answer to Peter's question. So, I made it up.

"It is said they had help on the outside, friends waiting with horses. They chose a time when the brass band and performers from the Fashion Theater made a commotion on the plaza and got everyone's attention. The sheriff's deputy did not discover the empty cell until much later."

"They got away?" one of the new diners asked.

"*Puede ser.* They might have."

"What do you mean?"

My imagination was running full tilt now, and I described to my attentive audience of three the pictures that formed in my mind.

"The sheriff and his deputy followed the trail, all the way to Laredo. Those cocky fellows stopped at a saloon for a drink before crossing the Río Bravo. The story goes that one drink led to two, then three, and soon they were too drunk to go anywhere."

"The sheriff found them!" Peter slapped his thigh and laughed out loud. "Back to the Old Bat Cave."

Peter could get into a story. That made the telling all the more fun.

Mamá called that the food was ready. She had ladled the steaming carmine mixture of chili con carne into earthenware bowls and heaped frijoles onto plates, framing them with a couple of rolled tortillas. The spicy aroma was mouthwatering. The men dug into the food voraciously as soon as Josefa set their bowls and plates on the table. I turned to Peter Meyer.

"Have more coffee. I'll tell you another tale."

"Thank you. The coffee is very strong—and it is late. I have to be at the store early tomorrow morning."

"Not yet!" I blurted out. I wanted him to stay a little longer. I was having too much fun. "How about a cigarette?" I retrieved the tin from near the coffee pot where I had placed it earlier. I made a show of opening it to reveal a row of cigarettes. "I made them myself."

He examined the smokes. All he said was, "Well, if you did, I must have one."

I removed a cigarette from the case and offered it to him. He placed it between his lips and waited for me to strike a match. I tried to light it with dash, the way I had seen Martha do. My hand shook a little, and on the third try I succeeded. Peter Meyer did not grow impatient or take the match from my hand. When the cigarette was lighted, he inhaled deeply and then released a puff of smoke.

"Very good," he said. "Very good. You know how to do many things, señorita Pérez. Now, I really must be going. How much do I owe you?"

"Five cents for the enchiladas, two cents for the coffee and two cents for the smoke. Nine cents."

He dropped several coins into my hand. "The extra is for your story—the one you embellished to entertain me." His smile lit up his face. His eyes twinkled.

I thought my chest might explode.

"Gracias," I curtsied as I had seen Martha do.

He tipped his hat, turned, and in rangy strides, walked away. The smoke from his cigarette slowly curled skyward in the humid air.

I watched him leave, excited by what had passed between us. I turned away from his receding figure toward the two men who were wiping the last drops of sauce from their bowls with the remnants of their tortillas. They ordered coffee and cigarettes. Josefa filled their cups, then held out her cupped hand. I handed over nine cents but kept my penny tip. A pittance. *It will take a long time to make enough tips to do what I want to do,* I thought. *I have to find a faster way.*

CHAPTER 5

"*Por lo tanto, usted cree que me puede ayudar.* So, you think you can help me?" Josefa huffed, her tone incredulous, her language formal. I braced myself because I had asked her to tighten my corset. I usually kept the corset laced in back. That made it easy to put on. All I had to do was fasten it in front with its hook and eye closures. But the laces had loosened with wear and needed adjusting.

"Help me! What makes you think that I need help?" She snapped and pulled my laces taut. "Too tight?"

"Just right," I lied. "Every night, Josefa, I see you working hard to make sure all the diners get what they order."

"Yes, and they get exactly what they want because I am careful. I do not hear any of them complaining."

They do not return, I thought but said, "The two of us working together can serve twice as many diners at once."

"We do not have more than I can handle."

"But what if we did? What if more people came to our stand?"

"*¿Por qué lo harían?* Why would they?"

"*Puede ser que*. They might," I tugged at my chemise, smoothing it as I pulled it down under the tight corset.

"What are you planning to do? Papá will not like it if you misbehave, Lupe." Josefa tossed me a small bustle pad.

"*¿Me porto mal?* Misbehave? Me?" I positioned the bustle pad behind and secured its ties in a flat bow just below my waist.

"You are cheeky, Lupita."

The comment annoyed me, and I turned to look my sister in the eye. "All I want to do is help. We could be more profitable every night. Other stands do more business than we do. At ten o'clock the other night, I counted more than twice the number of people at the stands of Jovita, Rosa, and Juanita than we had. Sometimes the difference is even larger. You know that Mamá's food is just as good as theirs—maybe even better—so why the difference? What do you think?"

"How can I know? While you are counting, I am waiting tables."

I slipped my arms through the sleeveless corset cover, nodding as I buttoned the garment. That was the difference. Josefa served while the other chili queens hosted, entertaining their customers with banter and sometimes song, telling tall tales, cracking jokes, and flashing beguiling smiles—selling more, earning more.

"I told you that I have been watching Martha," I said. "She has the most customers of any chili queen on the plaza."

Josefa was expressionless. She was tying her own bustle pad in place.

"Josefa, *escúchame*. Listen to me."

"You have my attention. Now, get to the point."

"Martha tells stories."

Josefa scowled. "I told you, Lupe, I do not know how to make up stories."

"You do not have to make them up. Martha gets them from her customers. I have heard her ask her diners, the ones from out of town, to tell her what has happened to them or about unusual things they have seen. She listens and saves their stories to tell another night to another audience."

"*¿Cómo sabes?* How do you know?"

"I have heard them told, and I have heard Martha repeat them. And they get better with retelling. Martha embellishes them. Her customers love it. I have even seen some return to hear her tell their own stories."

"And you think that you can do what she does?"

I ignored the derision in Josefa's voice.

"You know what else Martha does?"

Josefa rolled her eyes.

"You know Jesse, the one who sings and plays guitar on the plaza? Martha calls him over to her stand, and they sing together. The customers join in. Some throw coins at Jesse and slip tips to Martha. I know she's making money. We can do as well, Josefa, I know we can. Just let me. What is the harm in that?"

I was silent for a moment, hesitant about saying more. But Josefa wasn't warming to my argument. So, I decided to take a chance.

"There is something else. Martha does not dress the way we do. She wears a chemise with short sleeves and a petticoat shorter than the chemise, enough to show her ankles."

"Lupita!" Josefa's tone was scolding. "Mamá and Papá would never allow you to dress like that."

I understood her concerns. Chili stand vendors expected their daughters to walk a delicate line, to be entertaining and pleasant while guarding reputations as virtuous young women, even when customers became ardent. The chili queens who ran their own stands could be more flamboyant. Martha Garcia was one of my favorites. I wished I could be like her.

"Martha always has a shawl or rebozo with lots of fringes. She drapes it around her shoulders, and it slips and slides. You never see more than a patch of skin here and there, but it is flirtatious."

"¡Provocativa!" Josefa said.

I knew that I had gone too far. I returned to my original argument. "I can help bring in more customers, Josefa, I know I can. Give me a chance."

"*Lo voy a pensar*. I will think about it." Then Josefa added, "So long as you dress modestly and promise to do what I say."

"*Por supuesto*. Of course," I answered. I thought that I might have gained a foothold.

"Josefa! Lupita!" Mamá called.

Josefa had finished dressing while I was talking and I had not caught up. She frowned. "Hurry up. We have sauce to make."

I stepped into a floor-length skirt with its many folds of fabric and arranged its pleats over the bustle pad. Between us, Josefa and I had four skirts. There were two of cotton, the deep blue I had just fastened at my waist, and the maroon Josefa was wearing. For cooler weather we had two of wool, one brown and one black. We shared clothing, sewing extra buttons at closures to tighten or loosen the fit.

I rummaged through the trunk at the foot of our bed for a bodice. The trunk was deep, so soft, thin garments were usually buried under heavy, bulky ones. I pushed the woolen skirts aside, feeling under them for cotton bodices appropriate for the mild, humid weather. As I pulled out a white-and-blue-striped cotton, the back of my hand brushed against something silken. I turned my palm down so I could grasp the fabric, but it slipped away. I reached for it again, captured a section with thumb and forefinger, and gently tugged. A length of fabric emerged from the trunk, a pattern of bright vermillion stripes running lengthwise alongside dark, indigo ones, interrupted by various small sections of white. It was wide and very long. When I draped it around my shoulders, the delicately knotted long fringes on both ends touched the floor. I wore rebozos of cotton and wool as head coverings and draped about my shoulders for warmth and for accent color. I used them to carry bundles. Mothers carried their babies in them. But never before had I experienced the fine texture of silk next to my skin. This rebozo slipped across my arms with a movement all its own. I let it drape across my shoulders, cling to my breasts, and hug my arms and waist, its fringes dancing with my every turn.

"*Date prisa*, Lupita. We are waiting for you."

I returned the silk rebozo to the bottom of the trunk and hurriedly fastened my bodice, smoothing it in place. *Where did we get something this beautiful?* I wondered as I joined Mamá and Josefa in the yard.

"Mamá." She was mashing soaked ancho chile skins in a *molcajete*. The rough lava rock bowl was perfect for crushing and grinding tough-skinned chiles and garlic cloves.

"Sí," Mamá responded absently. She pressed the *tejolote*, the pestle, into the softened chiles.

"I found something in the trunk, something I had not seen before. It was in the bottom, beneath the other things. *Un rebozo de seda*. A silk rebozo, so fine that it slipped through my fingers."

Josefa looked up from her molcajete where she, too, was mashing anchos. "A silk rebozo?"

Mamá made an audible sigh. "Ah, *lo encontraste*. So, you found it. I had planned to share it with both of you. Later, we'll look at it together and I will tell you its story. First, we must make the sauce.

"Today, we will try my new recipe. But you must promise to keep it secret. Josefa tells me that you are worried about business, Lupita. This is one way to bring in more customers. No other chili stand on the plaza will have a sauce that tastes like the one we are about to make. Do you promise?"

"Sí, Mamá. Sí."

"Then watch me and listen."

Mamá placed a cloth packet on the table in front of us. Using the tips of her index finger and thumb, she peeled back the four corners that had been folded over one another to reveal slender chiles with wrinkled skin the color of dark raisins. "*Estos son chiles pasillas, la forma seca de las chilacas.* These are pasilla chiles, the dried form of chilacas," she told us.

"Where did you get them?" I asked.

"In Market Square. I bought them from señora Mendoza yesterday. They looked so pretty on the blanket she lays out to display the chiles she sells. I have not seen pasillas for some time now. They will help us make a distinctive sauce. And, if we are clever about it—and secretive—no one will be able to duplicate the taste of the Pérez chile sauce. It all depends on the proportions. We will use anchos for our base, as they are the sweetest and the most plentiful. Six anchos, half as many pasillas, and *guajillos.*"

Mamá showed us two bowls, one containing soaked and softened pasillas and the other, guajillo chiles. "I put these in warm water much earlier so they would be ready to use now. See how plump they are. They need to be stemmed and seeded. The anchos are mashed. As soon as you prepare the pasillas and guajillos, we can add them to the anchos. You know to be careful not to rub your eyes or nose with your hands once you have touched the chiles. These are not as hot as *chile piquin*, but their oils can sting. Keep them separated from one another. After you have prepared them, I will show you how to mix them with the anchos."

Josefa worked with the pasillas, and I with the smooth, shiny red guajillos.

"Mash them, moisten with water, and push them through the sieve," she directed.

As we each pressed our chile pulp through the sieve, thick purée dripped down into the bowl, leaving the tough skins behind. We discarded them.

"*Entonces.* Now," Mamá said, "we will combine the purées until we have the taste I want." And she directed Josefa to add the pasillas to the anchos, one-third of the mix at a time. After the addition of two parts, Mamá dipped the folded end of a tortilla into the ancho-pasilla purée mixture. She bit into the tortilla, closed her eyes, and savored the flavor. We waited. Mamá opened her eyes and motioned Josefa to add the remaining third left in her bowl. She tasted again, nodded, and smiled.

Now it was my turn. I added a third of my guajillo purée into the mix and waited for Mamá to taste. At her direction, I added another third, and finally the rest of the "little raisin" chiles.

"It is becoming a thick paste, Mamá."

"*Agregue agua, poquito a poquito.* Add water, a little at a time."

While we were doing that, Mamá crushed peeled garlic cloves she had roasted on the comal. She added the garlic to the purée, seasoning with salt. She gave me the task of rendering lard in a pan over the open fire to cook chopped onions translucent, added the chile purée to the onions, then diluted the thick mixture with water until it clung to a tortilla. She sprinkled in oregano and a little cumin, moving the pot away from the most intense heat to simmer the sauce for a few minutes.

Mamá tore off pieces of tortilla for each of us to use as tasting spoons. "Hold the sauce in your mouth. What flavors can you find?"

"Café," I said.

"A woodsy taste," said Josefa.

"That's the ancho talking. What else?"

"Berries," Josefa added. "I know where that comes from—the guajillos."

"And something different, like licorice," I said. "I taste licorice."

"You see what the pasillas offer?" Mamá smiled.

We went silent for a moment. Then began to giggle, united in our covert creation.

Mamá's smile and the slight jerk of her head told us that she was satisfied. "*Entonces podemos ver el rebozo.* Now, we can see the rebozo."

Salsa de Chiles
CHILE SAUCE

5 garlic cloves, unpeeled
6 dried ancho chiles, seeded and stemmed
3 pasilla chiles, seeded and stemmed
3 guajillo chiles, seeded and stemmed
1½ teaspoons salt
2 tablespoons lard or oil
1 cup chopped onion
½ teaspoon dried Mexican oregano
½ teaspoon cumin
Yield: 1½ cups sauce

This was Mamá's most distinctive chile sauce. She combined three different chiles that each contributed a unique flavor and spicy heat to the sauce.

Toast the garlic cloves over high heat in a large skillet, griddle, or comal. When the skins are charred on all sides, remove from the heat and cool. The garlic cloves should peel easily.

Rinse the dried chiles and place them in hot water, each type in a separate bowl. Be sure they are submerged. Soak them until they are soft.

Working with each type of chile separately, slice each down one side. Remove the stem and the ball of seeds. If you remove all the seeds and ribs, the sauce will be mild. Rinse the softened chiles. This will remove most of the heat from the peppers. Mamá made a sauce with moderately spicy heat, just enough to register at the back of the throat, so we did not remove all the ribs or seeds. But we removed most of the seeds. You will want to taste your chiles for spicy heat to adjust to the level you prefer.

Again working with each type of chile separately, mash the softened chiles. We used a *molcajete** to mash the chiles. Starting with the mashed anchos, add first the pasilla and then the guajillo chile purée to make a mixture of the three that suits your taste.

Mash the combined chile mixture with the garlic in the molcajete.*

Add 1½ teaspoons salt and 2 cups water, and blend.** Pour the mixture through a strainer into a bowl to collect as much of the purée as possible, then discard the skins left in the strainer.

Melt 2 tablespoons of lard or oil in a pan*** over high heat. Sauté the chopped onions until they are soft. Add all the strained chile purée in the bowl to the pan and stir until the onions and chiles are well combined. Add ½ teaspoon cumin and ½ teaspoon Mexican oregano. Add a little water and boil. Then reduce the heat and add just enough water to simmer into a thickened sauce. Dip the end of a tortilla into the sauce to test. If the sauce clings to the tortilla, it has the right consistency. If your sauce is not thick enough, make a paste of cornstarch and water and gradually add small amounts of the cornstarch paste until the sauce gains the desired body.

Taste the mixture. If it is bitter add sugar, a small amount at a time, until you have just the right balance of flavor and spicy heat.

Serve hot over tortillas for enchiladas, over chile rellenos, or at room temperature as a dipping sauce. We also used this chile sauce as the base for our chili.

*An electric kitchen blender works well here.
**If using a blender, use the purée function to thoroughly blend these ingredients.
***Use a nonstick frying pan.

CHAPTER 6

We followed Mamá indoors. She motioned us to sit on the bed and opened the trunk. Reaching down into its depths she drew out the rebozo, gently unfolding its length. She draped the colorful garment over her shoulders, turning this way and that, making the garment dance. Its delicate fringes skirted the dirt floor. I leaned forward to touch, but Mamá quickly pulled away. She scowled.

"*Nunca he visto nada tan fino*. I have never seen anything so fine. Where did it come from?" I asked.

"*Era de mi mamá*. It belonged to my mother. Your Uncle Francisco found it among her things after her funeral. He brought it to me because I am your abuela's oldest daughter."

"*Es hermoso*. It is beautiful," I said. "Do you think I could wear it some-time?"

"You cannot wear it, Lupita, until I do. I am older. Ahead of you."

"But I found it first."

Mamá admonished us, "First, you must hear its story."

She fingered the bright red stripes alternating with blue-black ones, ir-regularly broken by white here and there. The stripes extended to a foot-long section of vermillion and indigo diamond shapes on each end. Be-tween the woven diamonds were sections where long threads—unwoven threads—bridged the colorful weavings to knotted fringes of both colors. Mamá waited for our attention. When we gave it, she began:

"*Esto es lo que me dijo mi madre.* This is what my mother told me. Her family was originally from a village near San Luis Potosí, where skilled weavers worked their back-strap looms to create distinctive rebozos. Your *bisabuela*, your great grandmamá, was an accomplished weaver. She would tie off skeins of natural cotton or wool thread following patterns she had learned from master weavers. The white spaces you see here amid the colored stripes are the places that did not take the dye. She liked strong colors, brilliant reds from cochineal and deep navy blue from indigo. The dyes bled a bit into the tied-off area, giving the cloth a marbled look. See here where the threads took the indigo unevenly."

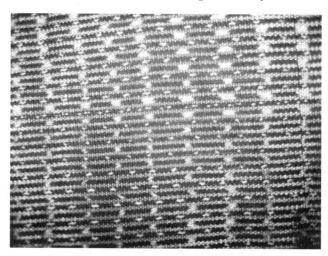

When the silk skeins for this rebozo were dyed, some of the dye bled into the tied-off areas. This made a distinctive pattern of irregular white spaces among the vermillion and indigo stripes. Mamá told me that the bleeding of dye into the white spaces was how you can tell that the rebozo was woven from yarn dyed in this way.
Photo of detail of silk rebozo in the collection of the Witte Museum, San Antonio, Texas.

"This is one of my bisabuela's weavings?" I asked.

"Let me finish the story, Lupita. You are impetuous."

"*Lo siento.* Sorry, Mamá." I wanted so much to know about this rebozo.

"Her textiles were well known, and she sold many to merchants who traded with vendors in Béjar. She did a good business, too. One day, a merchant brought her several skeins of silk thread and asked if she would weave a special rebozo for his bride. The quality of the silk was like none that she had used before, and she became determined to weave two—one for the merchant's bride and one for her own family. Your bisabuela bargained with him. She would weave the silk rebozo only for an equal quantity of the same silk thread.

"'That is out of the question,' he told her. 'The silk is too dear. I do not have access to unlimited quantities.'

"'I am not asking for an unlimited supply,' she said, 'just exactly what you brought me for one rebozo, enough so that I can make another.'

"The merchant resisted, offering your great grandmamá more money for her cotton and wool rebozos to pay for the preparation of the silk one. But she insisted on being paid in silk thread. If he could not find the thread, he would have to find another weaver, she told him. There was more haggling. She did not waver. Your great grandmamá knew how to bargain.

"The merchant relented on one condition. 'You must make my wife's rebozo different from any other.'

"To that, she agreed. She measured lengths of skeins to make the pattern you see in the rebozo, and dyed them. When she was satisfied with their colors, she threaded her loom and wove a rebozo, carefully knotting the long fringes in a unique design. Can you imagine how much skill and time that required? When the merchant returned for the silk rebozo, you great grandmamá told him, 'This rebozo is so supple that it will pass through your bride's wedding ring. It is like none that ever was or will be.'

"She dyed the silk she received as payment in much deeper shades of red and indigo and wove the threads into the singular pattern you see. The length of this rebozo lets you to wear it in many different ways: You can wrap it across your neck and let the ends dangle over your shoulders. Or cover your head with one end thrown over your shoulder and the other dangling in front. Or place the rebozo around your shoulders and under your arms to tie in the back. Drape it over your shoulders and across your bosom. The fringes will touch the hem of your skirt."

Mamá paused to let us try on the rebozo. She sat back to watch. "Your abuela told me that she and every one of her sisters were permitted to wear it, but only on special occasions," Mamá chuckled.

"*¿Qué te divierta, Mamá?* What amuses you, Mamá?" Josefa asked.

Mamá cocked her head and was silent for a long moment.

"*Dínos, por favor.* Tell us, please," I pleaded.

She responded in just above a whisper, "My mother told me that my grandmother knotted magic into the fringes. When you wear this rebozo, you can become whoever you wish to be."

"*¿Cómo?* How? How do you know?"

Mamá stoked the silken garment, smiling to herself.

"Mamá. How do you know?" I repeated, intent on shaking her loose from her reverie.

She raised her face toward us but she seemed to be looking beyond us. She was smiling. "You know that there were six daughters in the household and they all strove to be the most sought-after young women in the village."

"And?" I asked.

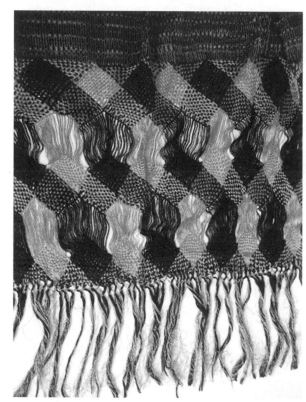

My great grandmama wove an intricate and distinctive pattern before knotting the fringes at the ends of our heirloom rebozo. Mamá said that is what gave the rebozo its magic.
Photo of border weaving detail on silk rebozo in the collection of the Witte Museum, San Antonio, Texas.

"You saw the fringes?"

We nodded.

"Well, all of them wore the rebozo at one time or another, and your great grandmamá boasted to everyone in their village who would listen that from the fringes of that rebozo, her daughters had hung the hearts of a hundred vaqueros."

Mamá half whispered, "This rebozo helped me to win the heart of one."

Josefa's voice rose in pitch, "You, also, Mamá?"

"¿Cómo?" I asked.

"My mamá was your great grandmamá's youngest daughter. She had been born many years after the other children and was the last to wed. She and your grandfather lived with bisabuela to care for her in her old age.

They inherited the rebozo and carried it with them to Tamulipas when your grandpapá took work on a hacienda in Cruillas. That is where I was born and grew up.

"Your father was young once, like you. And very good looking." Mamá smiled. "In his youth, he worked as a vaquero on the hacienda. He was an accomplished horseman. He was known as a *jinete*, one who could ride any horse anywhere. Many young women vied for his attention."

Mamá's face flushed. "I remember how he looked at the *charreada*, the rodeo. You should have seen the way he rode into the corral on his palomino stallion. He had raised Bravo from a weanling. He wore a white shirt and a large-brimmed black hat that sat squarely on his head. From the ends of its stampede straps dangled tassels made of Bravo's mane. His leather *montura*, his saddle, was intricately tooled by a master saddler.

"Your papá excelled in roping. He could jump from the back of his mount onto another running horse. I think he was best at doing tricks with Bravo. I remember how he would gallop toward the spectators. At first you thought he and Bravo would run right over you. But in a heart-pounding moment, Bravo's hind legs gained purchase, raising dust. With a chuckle, because he and Bravo had startled me, your papá raised his hat in greeting. Hardly touching rein, he signaled Bravo to turn. I can still hear the montura creaking—I always liked that sound—as the two moved like one being to the center of the corral. There, they entertained with roping tricks."

"I had no idea," Josefa said.

Mamá shook her finger at us. "You think of your papá as an old man, his skin weathered and lined, his hands roughed by hard work, crippled. In my memories, I can see him as he looked then, before living took its toll. He could stand on his horse's back and jump through twirling lasso loops. He left me breathless."

"And the rebozo?" I asked.

"I thought your papá was the handsomest young man I had ever seen, and I wanted him to notice me. At dances, many young women surrounded him. I was not brave enough to push my way forward. So I admired him from a distance.

"I was lovesick. I could not eat. My share of the housework did not get done properly or on time. Your abuela was trying to teach me how to weave some intricate patterns on the loom, but I could not concentrate. Little by little, she drew it from me. 'I see,' she said. I recall this as if it happened yesterday. Your abuela sat opposite me, her eyes searching my face. 'Are you certain that you wish the attentions of this young man?' she asked.

"'Oh, sí, Mamá. I have never been surer of anything,' I told her.

"'You must be certain.' She answered my unspoken question. 'Because I have a way to help you.'"

"'The rebozo?'" I guessed.

"Mamá nodded. 'You may wear the rebozo with magic woven into its fringes at the next promenade. With the rebozo about your shoulders, you will hold the ends so that you can control the movement of its fringes. You will find a place in the line of young women and walk past the young men moving in the opposite direction. You will find him in the line and focus on him, never letting your eyes or attention wander. As his path approaches yours, you will call his name. At the precise moment he turns toward you, flip the fringes at him and offer a compliment.'

"'What compliment shall I use?' I asked her. I was very young and unsure of myself. Your abuela put her hands on her hips and chuckled. She tilted her head and asked, 'He is an accomplished vaquero, proud of his skills. What do you think you could say to him?'"

"¿Qué pasó?" we chorused.

"At the promenade on the hacienda's main plaza the very next Sunday, I locked my eyes on your father and did not let go for a moment. I was afraid that I would miss my chance. I was so nervous. I almost forgot to flip the fringes at him. But the rebozo seemed to fly up without my help. It got his attention and my nervous hoarseness caused him to linger a moment, to lean toward me to hear my whispered compliment about his horsemanship. A smile was in his eyes and in his voice as he asked me to join him for a stroll. That was the beginning of our life together. Just as your grandmamá promised, this rebozo had cast its spell."

"What a lovely story, Mamá! May I repeat it?"

She shook her head. "This is my personal story. If you are looking for good stories to tell at the stand, Lupita, you should ask Papá. He can tell you how we got to the King Ranch and about his adventures driving cattle on the open range. He has many tales to tell—better than some you hear on the plaza."

Mamá tilted her head, a wry smile playing around her mouth. "*Sí*, Lupita. *Mucho mejor*, much better."

CHAPTER  7

He had thrown a shoe.

"*Lo llevaré*. I will take him," I heard Papá tell Mamá. "José will go with me."

"I need him to help carry firewood and lift my cook pots," Mamá said. "Take Lupita instead."

"*Tiene trabajo que hacer aquí*. She has work to do here."

"*Puede esperar*. It can wait. Take her with you. She wants to know your stories."

"¿Mis historias?"

"Sí, from the time we were *Kineños*, King's people." Mamá waved her hand, urging us away. "Josefa, José, and I can manage. ¡Vamos!"

Papá shrugged and handed me Caballo's halter and lead line.

Everyone just called him Caballo. He was an old bay gelding we shared with the neighbors. He obediently did all the jobs we asked of him, mostly pulling the loaded wagon to and from the plaza: kettles, barrels, earthenware, and foods for our chili stand.

Caballo's gait was slightly off because of one hoof, its wall torn where the nails had been wrenched out when he lost his shoe. We had to walk him slowly and watch the ground to avoid more serious damage. Sharp rocks could bruise his exposed hoof and cause laming abscesses. The slow pace suited Papá and gave us time to talk.

We headed north along San Pedro Creek toward John Illg's blacksmith shop on Presidio Street. The San Antonio Gas Company's smokestack was a familiar beacon.

Papá and I walked north along San Pedro Creek with Caballo, bound for John Illg's blacksmith shop on Presidio Street. You can see the blacksmith's shop in the background center of the photo. The smokestack on the left marks the location of the San Antonio Gas Company.

San Pedro Creek, copied from the original stereograph by Alexis V. Latourette, ca. 1877, General Photograph Collection, 362: 088-0320, University of Texas at San Antonio Libraries Special Collections from the Institute of Texan Cultures.

Caballo pulled on the lead line as we walked along the narrow, shallow San Pedro Creek, so we stopped to let him nibble on a small patch of grass. That's when I told Papá why I wanted to hear his stories.

Now fifty-three, Papá seemed old to me, his face lined and roughened by years of exposure to the unyielding sun of the Wild Horse Desert. Yet, what I had just said to him seemed transforming. He brightened. His dark eyes danced. For a split second, I saw a hint of what had been the handsome man of his youth.

"*Hay mucho que decir.* There is a great deal to tell," he said. "I was a vaquero for many years. What do you want to know?"

"*Todo*, Papá, your whole story, from as far back as you can remember."

As he talked, we stopped here and there so he could emphasize the recollections he treasured. Mamá was right. Papá's stories were better than those I had heard on the plaza. I listened intently, trying to commit to memory his every word.

We arrived at the blacksmith shop too soon for my liking. But Papá promised to tell me more later. I tied Caballo to the hitching post outside the barn-size shop with its massive front doors folded open against the building. We walked through the wide and tall opening into a spacious workplace. Natural light rayed through several large windows. Bright red sparks cascaded over the dirt floor from the brick forge where Antonio Ortiz was bent over a coal bin. He was stoking the open furnace that vented through the roof.

"¡Hola, Antonio!" I yelled above the fire's roar.

Antonio looked up, squinted, and nodded his recognition. His round face was smudged with soot and glistened with sweat. His barrel chest filled a dark cotton shirt that was too small, straining its seams. He had rolled its sleeves up to his elbows. A bibbed leather apron covered his stocky frame from midchest to boot. He wiped his brow on his sweat-stained sleeve and smiled.

"¿Qué pasó?"

"Caballo lost a shoe."

"When are you going to give that animal a real name?"

"¿Por qué? Caballo is a good name."

"It tells nothing about him, not his coloring, his temperament, his behavior, nothing at all, except that he is a horse."

"Lupe," Papá called, "*Traelo adentro*. Bring him in. Señor Illg says that Antonio will replace the shoe now."

I fetched Caballo from the hitching post, leading him to where Papá was talking with Antonio near the forge.

We clustered around the animal. He seemed to enjoy the attention. Antonio ran his hand down his legs and Caballo obediently lifted each hoof in turn for inspection.

"He is overdue for a trim," Antonio told us. "He has outgrown his shoes. Look here. See a nail is missing. If you had waited much longer, he would have thrown this one, too."

"*Hazlo entonces*. Go ahead, then," Papá said to the apprentice blacksmith. "Replace all four." To me he said, "We can walk to the plaza to purchase some chiles and vegetables for Mamá, then return to get Caballo. On the way, I can tell you more stories."

"¿Las historias?" Antonio was curious.

"You will have to come to dine at our chili stand to find out," I called to him over my shoulder as Papá and I walked away.

Papá did not disappoint. The next story he told was even better than the first ones. And he had more, he said, for yet another time. I had struck gold.

That evening as we set up for the night on the plaza, Josefa whispered to me, "I need to be away from the stand for about an hour. You said you wanted a chance to be the hostess. Take over tonight. Will you?"

I was stunned. I thought I would have to fight my sister to be hostess at our chili stand. Now, she was offering it to me—to be sure, for only a little while tonight—but offering it voluntarily. *Why would she do that?* "Where are you going?"

"To the Fashion Theater."

"To see Tom O'Malley?"

She nodded, smiling. I strained to hear her whispered reply, "If I can get to the theater early, before performances begin, he said he would introduce me to his friends. It is early in the evening. I doubt that you will have much work. José is still here. He can help you."

"What will you tell Mamá and Papá?"

"That Jovita on the other side of the plaza needs help—just a little fib. I will not be long. Will you do this for me?"

I hesitated, unsure if I should help Josefa in this ruse.

"Por favor, Lupe," she pleaded. Her voice became strained. "You can be chili queen while I am gone. That is what you want."

"I know, Josefa, but I think you are playing with fire."

"That is what is so exciting, Lupe."

The next moment, I caught sight of Peter Meyer only a few yards from our stand. My reservations about Josefa's judgment diminished with his each approaching step. "Go," I said and waved her off.

"¡Hola! Mr. Meyer. You are early tonight."

"Mr. Kotula asked me to pick up supplies coming in on the evening train. I thought I'd have a bite to eat before heading to the depot."

"Enchiladas? Tamales? Chili?"

"Chili tonight, with frijoles and tortillas and a cup of chocolate."

Mamá was staring at Josefa's back as my sister hurried away. I was glad to distract her with Peter's order.

"And something else," Peter said.

"¿Qué?"

"A story."

There it was. I could not have asked for a better request. I had the perfect one ready to deliver. I offered Peter his napkin and a spoon. We chatted for a few minutes until Mamá called. I set a bowl of chili before him with a plate of frijoles, fragrant in their spicy sauce, and two soft and lightly browned tortillas. I placed a single portion chunk of dark chocolate into a *chocolatero* and added hot water. When the chocolate was completely dissolved, I whisked it frothy by spinning the stem of the *molinillo* between my hands. I poured the hot drink into an earthenware cup. Peter said he liked his chocolate sweet so I added several teaspoons of *piloncillo*, stirred, and sprinkled some cinnamon on top. I began my tale as I set the drink before him.

Chili

2 pounds chopped, not ground, beefsteak or pork butt
6 cups chile sauce

The basis for our chili was our chile sauce. It was prepared with all the seasonings that made our chili distinctive. We filled a Dutch oven with the sauce, then added pieces of uncooked meat. We never cooked our meat before adding to the sauce. It cooked in the sauce so that it took on the chile flavors. To stretch the meat, use more chile sauce. This recipe will yield about 6 cups of chili. We multiplied the recipe depending on the number of chili orders we expected each night.

Place six cups of chile sauce in a pot. Dilute with just enough water to make it the consistency of a thick soup. Bring the sauce to a simmer over medium heat. Do not boil. Add the meat. Cover. Simmer over very low heat for several hours, until the meat flakes easily with a fork. If the chili needs thickening, add small amounts of a cornstarch and water paste until you have the desired consistency. If the chili is too thick, mix in small amounts of water to maintain the desired thickness.

Serve small bowls of chili with fresh tortillas and frijoles on the side.

Hot Chocolate

1 square of Mexican chocolate*
1 cup hot water
cinnamon to taste

Place the square of chocolate in a small bowl and add hot water. Let the chocolate melt. Using a molinillo**, beat the liquid until the surface becomes frothy. Pour into a cup and sprinkle with cinnamon.

Papá always took his chocolate unsweetened. He used to say that if you had to sweeten your cup, you had been served bad chocolate. He liked to taste the full flavor of rich dark chocolate. For my customers who preferred a mildly sweet drink, I would add a little raw honey to taste. For those with a sweeter tooth, we dissolved ground piloncillo grains in warm water and drizzled the syrup into the hot chocolate. Some diners preferred to add grains of piloncillo to their drink themselves for the degree of sweetness they desired.

*Mexican chocolate, available in most grocery stores, is typically sold in a solid or bar form and is shelved near tea, coffee, and other hot chocolate preparations. There are both imported and domestic brands. Make sure that the package is labeled Mexican chocolate, because it is different from American-style cocoa and hot chocolate preparations.

**A whisk may be substituted for a molinillo.

"*Estábamos Kineños.* We were King's People."

Peter's blue eyes looked questioningly over the rim of his cup.

"Sí, we came from the Wild Horse Desert in South Texas. I was born on the Santa Gertrudis division of the ranch."

"How long were you there?"

After melting Mexican chocolate in hot water and adding sugar, I inserted the bulb of the molinillo into the liquid and rolled the stem of the molinillo between my hands. The action rotated the bulb and made the surface of the drink frothy. I then sprinkled the froth with ground cinnamon and served the cup to Peter Meyer.

"For all my life, until a few years ago when we came here."

"Did your parents always live there?"

"No. They came from a hacienda in Cruillas in the state of Tamulipas, Mexico. When a bad drought struck there, Papá said that many cattle perished. One day in the year that Mamá and Papá married, Captain Robert King arrived and purchased the surviving longhorns, leaving all on the hacienda without work."

Peter scowled. "That was not good."

I shook my head. "Papá told me that Captain King offered the vaqueros work on his ranch, so they gathered their families, their horses, and their possessions and followed the herd across the Río Bravo to the Wild Horse Desert.

"They built everything, the corrals, their *jacales*, even a cabin for Captain and Mrs. King. Daily work was with longhorns and mustangs. Papá was a skilled vaquero. He did not mind the hard work. In fact, to hear him say, he was happiest when in the saddle, following herds out onto the grazing lands, rounding up, cutting and branding the new calves. But it was horses that he prized, the mustangs that roamed free on the desert that he helped to capture and tame. Papá became the head wrangler."

"Sounds like a hard life."

A voice answered from behind me. "It was not easy, but I loved it."

I introduced José and Peter to one another.

Peter said to him, "You sound as if you miss the place."

"I do. I wish more with each passing day to be back on the Wild Horse Desert. Before my father had his accident, I thought I would become a vaquero. I was learning the skills on the King Ranch. My papá was teaching me and the other vaqueros were, too—some of the most accomplished horsemen and cattlemen in all of Texas. But here in San Antonio, the best I can hope for is to be a day laborer and to help at this stand."

"Why did you like the vaquero life?" Peter asked.

"When you are a vaquero, you have your own *remuda*, your own tack, your own lasso, gun, and knife. You care for and ride your own horse and work the herds. Vaqueros face danger every day. That is why they are respected."

"You want respect."

"Of course. Every man does. But it is more than that. I want to live outdoors and in the saddle with other men I admire—on the ranch, in camp, and on the range. I want to see new places and have adventures. I want to go on trail drives. I want to be somebody important, a man others admire."

"I would like to know about those adventures," Peter said, taking a bite of his tortilla.

I saw my chance and was about to tell the story I had heard at Sadie Thornhill's stand when Josefa returned. "Come back tomorrow," I said to Peter, "to hear an amazing tale of a cowhand in disguise on the open range."

"A bandit on a trail drive?"

I shook my head.

"A spy from another trail drive?"

I shook my head again.

"What other reason could there be for a disguised cowhand?"

"Come back tomorrow," I repeated. "My story will surprise you. And bring your friends."

CHAPTER 8

At about six the next evening, Tom O'Malley arrived. Josefa's cheeks flushed as he kissed her hand. She held it in his for a long moment before inviting him to meet Mamá and Papá, who appeared stiff by comparison to the easygoing Mr. O'Malley. I saw them exchange questioning glances. Josefa was completely absorbed with the actor. So much so, that she tacitly allowed me to take the role she had been so reluctant to share before he entered her life.

A couple of passersby recognized the redhead and stopped to greet him.

"Mr. O'Malley," one said. "Will you honor us with a song?"

"I'd be happy to," he said, "after I finish eating. Sit down and have a plate of enchiladas or a bowl of chili. They make the best sauce on the plaza at this stand. You won't find better elsewhere." He winked at Josefa and smiled at me.

Couples and individuals, families and friendship groups, milled about the plaza. Some gathered around one of the troubadours singing a ballad about unrequited love. A couple purchased candy from el dulcero. Señor Hernández had extended his hours on the plaza to test evening sales. Others were browsing vendors' wares. A peddler was selling serapes.

The people Tom O'Malley had invited to stay took places on the bench. "Please, miss, we'll have what he's having," they said.

Just as I was serving them, Peter Meyer arrived with a fellow boarder from Mrs. Porter's house on the plaza's south side.. "I've come to hear the story about the disguised cowhand. Doubting Emile here thinks your story is probably pure fiction. I brought him along so he could judge for himself—and have a bowl of your tasty chili."

"A disguised cowhand?" Tom O'Malley said. "I have to hear that one."

Their comments piqued the interest of others milling near the stand. I saw the curiosity in their expressions. I took a deep breath and began, "Oh, it is true, all right. I heard it from the trail boss Mr. James Johnson." It was the story I had heard at Sadie's stand.

A cowboy wearing a hat cocked at a jaunty angle, its brim turned up on one side, stopped in his tracks and tentatively took a step toward our stand. "Ma'am, did you speak the name of James Johnson?"

"Sí, do you know him?"

"Worked fer him on the open range."

"Then hear me. You may know this story."

He tipped his hat revealing dark brown hair and serious brown eyes in an open tanned face, and sat on a bench near the others. "I'll have a plate of those enchiladas while I listen," he said.

Business was picking up.

After I served him he took a bite, chewed and swallowed. His eyes widened. "Muy delicioso, señorita. Just a lil' kick from the heat," he said.

A blue-eyed friend who had shadowed the cowhand to the stand slid onto the bench beside him.

"We got another buddy who's gone fer a drink. Save a place for Jess, Bronco," he said to his pal. "Me llamo Ben," he told me. "My friend here is called Bronco 'cause he tames the wild 'uns. Most of the time he acts like one of 'em. He's a good man on the trail, but he's loco sometimes, 'specially after a few drinks. That's how he got his nickname."

Bronco cocked his head and shot me a crooked smile. "You're a good lookin' gal," he said.

"And we serve delicious chili. I guarantee that you have never tasted a sauce like ours . . . made from a secret recipe," I half whispered. I waited a moment, hands on hips. "Well, Bronco, one thin dime will get you a plate of chili with frijoles on the side. What do you say?"

Bronco elbowed his friend, winking at me. "¿Cómo te llamas?"

"Me llamo Lupe."

"*Bueno, Lupe, traigame chili con carne, frijoles, tortillas, y un tas de café, por favor.*"

While I was setting plates and cups for the two cowhands, Jess joined them. He asked for the same.

Ben piped up. "He can eat later. How about that story?"

"Yes. We're waiting, señorita Pérez," Peter said.

I began again.

"It had been a long, hard trail drive. Cattle stampeded. There were days between fresh water. And to top it all, Mr. Johnson had to fire some men for bullying a young hand. Now shorthanded, the trail boss had been doubling as a cowhand. When they neared Clayton, New Mexico, they set up camp and the boss went to town to see if he could find some trail men, Kansas men—the hands who hired on for drives to that state. When he got there, he heard about a young man looking for work at the livery stable."

Bronco looked up. "Livery stable's a good place to find good hands."

I nodded. "Turns out the boy had his own pony and was experienced with horses. Mr. Johnson hired him on the spot, took him to camp, and put him with the horse herd. He was a hard worker. He would get up on the darkest stormy nights and stay with the cattle, singing to them, until the storm was done. He was good-natured, modest, never used cuss words or tobacco, and always pleasant."

Ben whistled.

"His name was Willie Matthews, nineteen years old, from Caldwell, Kansas.

"Everything went fine for several weeks.

"They got to Hugo, Colorado, a little town on the Kansas Pacific Railroad, near the Colorado and Wyoming line. There was good grass and water, so they pulled up about a halfmile from town and set up camp."

Jess slapped Ben on the back. "Remember when we'd bed the herd for the night? If the weather was good, those were some of the best times we had together."

"Go on," Tom O'Malley said to me. "I want to hear about the disguise."

"Well, after dinner, the boy went to the trail boss and asked if he could quit. He insisted, he said, because he was homesick. The boss reluctantly let him go.

"At sundown, the men were all sitting around camp. The herd was settled on the bed ground. The boss looked up toward town and saw a lady, all dressed up, walking slowly toward camp. 'Boys, we are about to have female company,' he told the hands. He wondered why a woman would be walking to a cow camp, seemingly coming out of nowhere. Always a gentleman, he rose to receive her, waiting for her approach. All the men's eyes were set on her and every man was holding his breath. When she got within a few yards of the boss, she began to laugh and said, 'You do not know me, do you?'"

I was suddenly aware of a larger group of people now clustered around the men on the benches, standing, listening intently. They seemed to be hanging on my every word. One leaned toward her neighbor and whispered something. Her face was animated. I thought she might have figured out the boy's identity.

"For a moment, the trail boss was speechless. The young woman reached her hand out to him to shake and he said, 'Kid, is it possible that you are a lady?'

"'Yes.' She smiled. "I'm Willie—Wilhelmina Matthews.'

"The men all crowded around Willie and shook her hand, but they were dumbfounded and could hardly think of anything to say to her. One of the men got a wood box from the chuck wagon for her to sit on.

"'Now, I want you to explain yourself,' the trail boss said.

"'Well, my papa was an old-time trail driver from South Texas. He drove from Texas to Caldwell, Kansas in the '70s. He liked the country around Caldwell. On the last trip he made, he went to work on a ranch up there and never returned to Texas. That's where he met my mother. When I was a little girl, I used to hear papa talk a lot about the old cow trail. I made up my mind that when I was grown, I was going up the trail if I had to run off.

"'I read in the paper that big herds were passing near Clayton. So I thought, now is my chance to get on the trail. I saddled my pony, borrowed a suit of my brother's clothing and a pair of his boots. I told him I was going out into the country and that I might be gone for a while. 'Tell Papa not to worry about me,' I said. 'I'll be back.'

"'After a four-day ride, I was in Clayton looking for a job. I'm glad I found you to make the trip with, for I have enjoyed it. But I'm homesick. That old train can't run fast enough for me when I get on it.'

"The train left Hugo at 11:20 that night. One man stayed with the herd and the rest took Willie to town to see her off. They were truly sorry to see her go.

"Months later, after delivering the cattle, the trail boss returned to his ranch on the Pecos River. Waiting for him were two letters, one from Willie and one from her father. They thanked him for his kindness to her and invited him to visit them anytime.

"Willie was the only woman Mr. Johnson knew who had made a trip like that. She was a skilled hand, good with cattle and horses. She was dependable and well mannered. He wished that he had more like her—an all-around hand that any trail boss would be happy to have."

"That is an amazing story," Peter said. "You sure it's true?"

"I could not have made that one up, no matter how good my imagination."

I folded my arms across my chest. I felt quite pleased with myself.

Tom O'Malley stood and spoke while the crowd was still quiet. He had a keen sense of timing. "This young lady has charmed us with a delightful story. Show your appreciation." They clapped their hands and stamped their feet. A few whooped and hollered. I curtsied. Tom O'Malley held up his hand. The din faded. "It's almost curtain time at the Fashion Theater. I have to join the cast now, but in thirty minutes, you can have four hours of the best vaudeville show in town for one thin dime. Just walk across the plaza after your meal here. You'll have a night to remember."

Tom O'Malley swaggered off toward the Fashion Theater. Josefa seemed captivated by his departing form, unaware that our stand's benches were filling with eager customers.

"That was a good story," Peter said.

"I have more to tell. My father was head wrangler on many trail drives from the King Ranch, supplying cattle to Indian reservations and to buyers in many places. Lots of loco things happened on the open range," I told all within earshot.

"I'll return for more," he said, paid for his meal, added his usual tip. Emile did the same, then left with Peter.

"Bronco thrives on trail drives," Ben said, "but me? Let's jist say that I don't plan to trail cattle all my life. I wanna be a horse trader, buyin' and sellin' good horses, here in Texas and across the plains. If I kin git a good stallion and some nice mares, I kin breed my own stock. I'm gonna git my own spread."

"You'd better hurry, then." The deep voice belonged to a middle-aged man in a suit and shirt with starched collar and a four-in-hand tie. He wore a felt cowboy hat, its crown creased and its brim shaped by a master hatter. "Land's getting harder to come by. The open range is closing fast." He turned to face me. "Young lady, I would like a plate of what these boys seem to be enjoying so much."

The conversation at the table was lively. Now a couple took seats and called over some friends.

"What do you recommend?" one young man asked Bronco.

"Cain't go wrong with what I'm havin'. Chili con carne, frijoles, tortillas y café."

"I'll have what he's eatin'," the young man called out to me.

"Señorita, can you make enchiladas?" another asked.

"Oh, I'd like some enchiladas, too," a woman wearing a feathered hat said as she found a place to sit. "With a cup of chocolate, please."

I looked around for help. Josefa was nowhere to be found. Papá and José must have left without my seeing. Mamá was patting out tortillas as fast as she could. She nodded and smiled at me. But I could not remember who had ordered what. *I need help*, I thought.

Then Elena appeared.

Enchiladas

1 tablespoon lard or oil
10-12 corn tortillas
½ cup crumbled Mexican white cheese, such as queso fresco
½ cup chopped onion
chile sauce

Enchiladas were a mainstay at our chili stand. At half the price of chili and frijoles, they were a favorite of families.

Heat each tortilla by placing in an oiled hot pan, or on a comal or grill. Heat one side for 30 seconds and quickly flip the tortilla over to heat the other side for an additional 30 seconds. The tortillas should be heated through but not burned.

Roll up the cooked tortilla or fold it in half, loosely. Place three rolled or folded tortillas on a plate. Pour hot chile sauce over the tortillas. Sprinkle crumbled queso fresco and chopped onions over the tortillas and serve.

CHAPTER 9

"Hola, Lupe. *Tu estás ocupado esta noche.* You are busy tonight."

"Oh, Elena. *Estoy muy contento de verte. Necesito ayuda.* I need help."

"Of course. Anything. What can I do?"

I wanted to hug her. Elena Hernández was my neighbor. She befriended me soon after we arrived in San Antonio. She was fun to be with, blessed with an effervescent personality. When she smiled, her large dark eyes danced. Elena lived every moment with exuberance. I liked that in her.

"I'm hungry," one of the men called out. "Señorita, please bring my plate."

"Un momento, señor."

I had enough of my wits about me to give Elena directions. She got to work, and I began serving chili to those I thought asked for chili.

"What does a body need to do to get served here?" a testy voice shouted.

"In a moment, señor."

"Young lady, are you going to serve us?" the woman in the feathered hat called out.

Flustered, I paused to try to regain my composure. Then I heard it, a distinct whirring sound overhead. A rope's large loop blurred past. I felt it pin my arms. My balance was compromised but I did not fall. My eyes followed the line of taut rope to my assailant. Bronco was tugging at the lasso.

"And y'all said I couldn' do it," he said to a man wearing a vest and string tie who was standing next to him. "I win."

I was trying to shake loose from the rope when my peripheral vision caught motion at some distance to my right. Another loop came flying from that location, but it wasn't headed my way. In seconds it encircled the cowboy who had lassoed me. His grip relaxed, the loop loosened, and I wriggled free.

"Now, what'd ya do that for?" the cowboy shot at his attacker. "We're jist havin' fun."

Antonio yanked the lasso. "You are bothering the señorita," he said.

"Aw! This fellow," he nodded to a man nearby, "he bet me two bits—that I couldn't lasso that gal in one throw."

"You're bothering the señorita," Antonio repeated.

"It was jist in fun," Bronco protested.

"You made a bet."

"So? Don't y'all ever bet?"

"Sí, but not at a señorita's expense."

"I didn' bet *with* her."

"You bet on her, that is worse."

"Aw, come on."

"Apologize to her."

Bronco turned to me. "Did I offend ya, ma'am?"

All the benches at our stand were now occupied. All the people on them were watching, wondering if there would be a fistfight. Time seemed to stand still. I felt numb, not knowing what to do. Elena grabbed my hand and whispered something but I did not understand.

"*Ellos van a pelear.* They are going to fight," Elena was saying. "*Se rompen todo.* They will break up everything."

"Well," Bronco's embarrassment had turned to defiance, "if I didn' offend 'er, what's there to 'pologize fer?"

Antonio wasn't satisfied. "Let her answer."

"For goodness sake, Lupita," Elena urged. "Say it is all right."

"You scared her," Antonio accused the cowboy. "*Pero no me asusta.* But you do not scare me." He yanked harder on the rope.

Bronco lunged at Antonio and fell, restrained by the lasso. Jess pulled a knife to cut the loop. The freed cowboy scrambled to his feet and dove at the waiting Antonio. People jumped up from their seats as the fighters crashed into one of the tables. Plates slid off the tabletop, splashing chili sauce over its cloth. A tin lantern overturned, skittering off the table onto the ground. Elena moved quickly to kick dirt over the flame and spilled kerosene.

Diners from nearby stands and passersby joined our customers. They gathered in a semblance of a semicircle to give the fighters some room and cheered on their favored contestant. Some in the crowd made bets on the outcome.

Bronco staggered to his feet, blood streaming from his nose. Antonio swung an arm at him, fist gripped in a tight knot. The punch he threw from this shoulder landed hard on Bronco's chin. The blow rocked the big man, but not enough to fell him.

The fighters circled one another, looking for a vulnerable place to strike, waiting for the moment when the other was off guard. Bronco moved first, rushing Antonio, lifting him off his feet. Antonio pummeled Bronco's back to no avail. Bronco began to spin with Antonio hoisted over his shoulder. He increased speed as Antonio flailed the air and punched Bronco's back. But Antonio could not free himself—until he bit down hard on Bronco's upper arm.

Bronco howled and dropped Antonio. His shirt was rent where Antonio had attacked with his teeth. The big man clutched his arm.

Antonio crouched down, and drew something from his boot. I caught its glint.

I jumped the overturned table, arms held high, and palms paddling the air.

"*Por favor. ¡Parada! ¡No más peleas!* Please stop before you kill one another."

I stood between the glowering men, arms stretched out as if to hold them apart, though I was not touching either.

"*¿Me oyes? ¡No más!* Hear me? No more!"

I turned to the spectators. "The show is over. This stand is closed. Come back tomorrow."

I turned to Jess and Ben. "Take Bronco away, please."

Jess slapped Bronco's hat on his head. Blood trickled through Bronco's torn sleeve.

"Take care of that."

Ben nodded and guided the stunned Bronco away.

I looked around for Antonio. He was brushing off his clothes and regaining his composure. Elena picked up his hat where it had fallen, dusted it off, and handed it to him.

I heard her say, "Tú eres valiente."

"He could have gotten himself killed."

"I mean you, Lupe, you are the brave one. I could not have stopped them like you did."

I put my hand to my pounding heart, closed my eyes, and said a silent prayer of thanks to our Lady of Guadalupe. I turned to Elena.

"Thank you for helping me."

"What about me?" Antonio said.

"You're loco."

"No gratitude?"

I was about to scold him when I noticed a red trickle from his nose.

"*Estás sangrando.* You are bleeding," I said.

Antonio wiped the back of his hand across his upper lip and sniffed. Elena offered him her handkerchief.

Antonio smiled and waved her away. He looked at the red streak on his hand and shrugged his shoulders. "Just a small cut."

"You were wonderful," Elena told him.

Antonio beamed and turned to me. "I look out for you."

"I know, Antonio. I appreciate that. But next time, please do not pull a knife." Antonio was well intentioned but brash. I did not want my fledgling audience to associate him with our stand. He might attract the roughest and frighten off some of the best. He shrugged and sat on a bench.

"Well, do I get some enchiladas for my trouble?"

Elena prepared a plate for him. He dug in.

I turned to Elena, "What brought you here tonight?"

Elena nodded toward a basket she had placed under one of the tables. "I was bringing Papá more candies for his tray. He told me that business has picked up since he began selling after dark. He has sold more candies in one night than in two afternoons on the plaza. Chili stand diners seem to like a sweet treat after a spicy meal."

"I hoped they would."

"Papá says that he is doing better because he has no competition at night."

Mamá came forward from the cooking place at the back of the stand. She surveyed the damage and shook her head. "We have to get this mess cleaned up. Be thankful tomorrow is Sunday. *Ayúdame, la, por favor.* Antonio, please help. *Vamos a ir a trabajar.* Let's get to work."

I began picking up the many shards strewn on the ground.

"They broke our earthenware. We will need to borrow some plates and cups until we can replace the broken ones," Mamá said.

"I think we can help," Elena answered. "I will ask my mamá."

"*Gracias*, Elena." Mamá smiled at her.

"Fortunately, the tables and lanterns just need minor repairs," Antonio said. "I can do that."

"*Necesitamos más*. Repaired tables and borrowed earthenware alone are not enough," Mamá said, and addressed me: "Why did it get out of hand, Lupe?"

I thought back to the events of the evening, trying to reconstruct what had happened.

Antonio offered his opinion. "I think, señora Pérez, that I got a little hotheaded."

"You were trying to defend me."

Many cowhands ate at our chili stand. The three shown here on Veramendi Street in front of Decker's Beer Garden were involved in the ruckus that unnerved me. That experience helped me learn about taking charge.
Cowboys on Veramendi Street, San Antonio, Texas, 1884-86, General Photograph Collection, 469: 083-0088, University of Texas at San Antonio Libraries Special Collections from the Institute of Texan Cultures.

"Sí, Lupita," Mamá said. "He saw you troubled by that cowboy. You needed to take control. If you are going to be hostess of a stand that attracts all types of people, drunk and sober, rough and refined, you need to be able to handle any situation that comes up. Not just for you, but for your customers, too."

This was the first time Mamá had acknowledged my role as hostess. I was pleased. But I also heard her criticism. Josefa had not had to deal with boisterous clients because she always served so few. I had attracted a crowd, among them a few rowdy men.

Mamá continued, "*Trata de recordar.* Try to remember. What was going on when things went wrong, Lupita? What could you have done to set it right?"

"*Me confundí.* I got confused," I said.

"*¿Demasiadas órdenes para recordar?* Too many orders to remember?" Mamá suggested

I nodded.

"How can we fix that?"

"*También.* Well, I guess that I cannot take care of so many customers by myself."

"Bueno. What else?"

Mamá gave me time to think but I did not know the answer to her question. She offered one. "Our customers were getting restless because we could not serve them fast enough and there was nothing interesting happening until Bronco lassoed you. And then it got exciting when Bronco asked if he had offended you and you did not respond."

"Well, he had. What could I say?"

"You could have said something to relieve the tension of the moment, something like, 'Well, you startled me, but I have been lassoed before' or 'I know that you did not mean me any harm' or simply, 'It is all right, Bronco.'"

"And then what do I do?"

"Regain the attention of your audience."

"How?"

"By getting them to think about something else, something that comes from you so that you become the center of their attention again."

CHAPTER 10

I lit a candle to Our Lady of Guadalupe at our *altarcito*, our home altar, and after Sunday Mass I knelt before her likeness at San Fernando. I bore her name and felt a special bond to her. I silently prayed, asking Our Lady to bless me, to help me earn the title of chili queen.

After Mass, we went home to prepare Sunday dinner, always a boisterous, busy, and cheerful event at our house. Papá sat at the head of a long table in the yard we shared with the Hernández family. Another table crossed the foot of Papa's table, forming an inverted *T*. Chattering grandchildren crowded on benches there, while my older brothers and brothers-in-law talked over one another up and down the length of Papá's table. My toddler nieces and nephews hung on the skirts of their mothers or ran erratically on wobbly legs. Sometimes they collided before tumbling in the dirt yard. Then there were tears and skinned knees. But the injured babies were quickly comforted and quieted by one of the adults.

The women served the men before joining them. Each looked after her husband and children, making dinner service manageable. Señora and señor Hernández and Elena usually helped and ate with us on Sundays, as they had no relatives living nearby.

Today, we enjoyed a spicy *puchero*, a stew that Mamá created from some soup bones we bought from the butcher. She added an assortment of leftover vegetables the produce vendors sold for reduced prices at the close of business on the plaza. Mamá served the stew with plates of chopped cilantro, sliced jalapeño, and lime quarters, so that each of us could season our stew as we wished. The puchero stretched far to feed our large family and the friends Papá often invited to join us. There were plenty of tortillas to go around, too. No one left the table hungry.

While the women cleared the table, the men helped stoke the fire and fill and lift pots to prepare hot water. I usually entertained with a story before dishwashing began. But today Mamá excused me from both jobs with, "*Ve a hablar con Papá.* Go talk with Papa."

I found him settled in his favorite chair under the old live oak in the yard, working in his mouth the cigar he saved for Sunday afternoons.

"Papá," I said. "*¿Compartirá más de sus historias?* Will you share more of your stories?"

He puffed, exhaling a series of perfect smoke rings. When we were small, we would try to put our fingers through the rings before they disappeared, and Papá would puff out more for us to poke. I stabbed one with my index finger. Papá smiled and motioned me to sit on a stool near him.

"I will tell you about lightning storms, crossing swollen rivers, rounding up stampeding cattle and horses, and passing through Indian reservations. I met Quanah Parker, you know."

I shook my head. "I did not know that, Papá. What was he like?"

Papá raised his hand to hush me. "*Te lo diré.* I will tell you all about my experiences on the old cattle trails—all, in time. They are good stories. Your customers will enjoy them—if you make them real in the telling. First, you must listen."

He began. One by one, as the cleanup work was done, family members gathered around to listen with me. We were surprised to learn what an interesting life our father had as a vaquero and head wrangler on the King Ranch. His face brightened as he recounted his memories of the open range. He looked younger, vigorous, when recalling times past. I wondered why he had left that life and was about to ask when he signaled an end to the storytelling.

"*Eso es todo para hoy.* That is all for today." To me he said, "Lupita, there is more to tell but you may not remember everything if you hear it all at once. We will resume another time. For now, think about what I have said and weave your stories."

"Sí, Papá. I am grateful. Gracias." I rose.

"Wait," Papá said. "There is something else I must say to you." He waved the others away.

I sat down again. He lowered his voice.

"Mamá tells me that you had some trouble controlling rowdy customers.

Do you remember what I told you about working with horses?"

"That was so long ago, Papá, when we lived on the King Ranch. Besides, I am not likely to work with horses here."

"I know that," Papá smiled and patted my cheek. "That is not what I meant. You can learn a lot from horses, Lupe. Groups of people can also behave like horse herds. Some individuals want to be the center of attention and to control. Others are content to follow the leader. As hostess, you must be the boss mare.

"You have watched with me the behavior of horse herds. Remember the time we saw the lead mare push away yearling colts that were acting up, fighting, and bothering the others? She made them understand that they could stay with the group only if they were well behaved. Those who continued to cause trouble were evicted. The other herd members helped her keep them away until they calmed down. You may not be able to change the behavior of rude ones, but you can divert attention away from them to you."

"¿Cómo?"

"The way you do in a corral. Show that you are in charge by your behavior and your presence. Stand tall. Square your shoulders. Command attention. Be clear and firm, and do not retreat. Keep pressure on the troublemakers until they stop. You must be a strong leader. Never waver, even when you feel uncertain. Select a path and stay on it. And expect people to follow you."

"What can I do if they do not?"

"Insist. If they persist, tell them to leave. Push them away from the group, the way the boss mare does with fractious colts. The others will help you."

"Gracias, Papá, *recordaré*. I will remember."

"And one more thing." He paused to puff on his cigar. "When you tell a story, keep the audience interested."

"I try."

"It is not good enough that the story interests your listeners. They must live in it. Keep them involved."

While I was mulling his advice, I felt a garment drape around my shoulders. I looked down to see the flutter of long indigo and vermillion fringes cascading onto my lap. I touched their silky beauty. *El rebozo!*

"*Lleve esto*. Wear this. It will give you confidence," Mamá said. "And the stories will come."

Tears welled. My parents were giving me their blessings to be chili queen at our stand and the means to become a good one. Our Lady of Guadalupe had answered my prayers. I said another silent prayer to her, this time of thanks.

That night, I lay awake inventing a character to take Papá's place in his stories, someone who would appeal to my customers. I had fun thinking up a name for him: Miguel Martinez. But I also worried a little about whether Josefa would resist.

There was no need. On Monday night, while we were setting up the stand, Josefa whispered in my ear, "I want to leave around half past seven. Can you take over?"

I turned to face her. "I know where you are going."

"Please, Lupe, promise not to tell."

"To the Fashion Theater. To see Tom O'Malley!" I added.

She smiled. "He is exciting. He is like no one I have ever met before." Her cheeks colored.

"Are you sure that is a good idea, Josefa?" I was torn. On the one hand, Josefa's interest in Tom O'Malley meant that she was relinquishing to me the role of hostess, the title that she had not wanted to share before he arrived. And his presence in her life seemed to make her happy. She glowed whenever she talked about him. On the other hand, Josefa, although older than I, was more innocent. Tom O'Malley was a man of the world. I did not want her to get hurt.

"What will I do if we are busy?"

"Elena wants to help. I asked her to come by around seven."

"What about Mamá and Papá?"

"I will explain to them—later."

I shook my head.

"Por favor, Lupe. I beg you."

Her large eyes were moist and her expression pleading.

"Bueno," I said. "But promise me you will be careful. Do not lose your heart."

Josefa embraced me and whispered, "I think I already have."

Dependable Elena arrived before Josefa left. Peter took a seat only moments later.

"Hola, señorita Pérez," he smiled his greeting. "I came back for your tasty enchiladas—and another story." His blue eyes twinkled. I suddenly felt bold. I called out to a man and woman who looked lost—tourists perhaps—standing nearby. "Would you like to hear my story, too?"

I beckoned to them. Elena was serving Peter enchiladas when they took their seats on the bench near him, eyeing his plate.

"They are very good," he told them.

"Only five cents a plate," I added. Both nodded.

Elena called their orders to Mamá, and took additional ones from a couple of men who joined them at our stand. I turned my back to our patrons momentarily while Elena served. I carefully pulled the silk rebozo from the carrying bag Mamá had crocheted. Slowly, I turned to face my audience, and with a flourish draped the garment over my shoulders. I opened and spread my arms full length like eagle wings to display the rebozo. The fringes fluttered. That got their attention. And so I began:

"Miguel Martinez was a skilled horseman in charge of the remuda, the working horses at the King Ranch. He moved the horse herds on many a trail drive from Texas to Kansas. And so many cattle! Numbering thousands. Many men were needed to drive them.

"The King Ranch had a special way of keeping track of men and animals alike—by the color of the animals' coats. All the hands tending a color group of cattle rode horses with similar coloring. Cowhands riding pintos drove paint cattle. If you rode a bay, your tended the brown ones. Chestnut ponies were used with the red herds. Just imagine what that looked like. Can you see them on the open range? Thousands of cattle and ponies in matching colors. Can you see it?"

I paused for a moment to give them time to picture it. The scene was vivid in my mind's eye.

"Keeping the horses in good order was Miguel's job. He also helped with the cattle. A never-ending job. He slept in all his clothes, in shirt, pants, boots, and, sometimes, even his spurs. Never knew what might happen. He was always ready. Any day. Any night. Anytime.

"Then it happened. About four o'clock on an April afternoon, it began to rain. All evening, all night. And the cold! It was bone chilling. Every man felt it. Every horse the men rode that bitter night, suffered. Those that survived needed weeks to recover.

"Cattle drift before wind-driven rain, and they stampede in thunderstorms. Lightning crashed around them that night."

A trio of cowhands had taken seats at the stand. One said, "Nothing can drill fear into a man's heart like those lightning storms on the open range."

"Then you know what Miguel felt," I said.

"Yes, ma'am. Sure do."

"Midnight. That's when the worst of the storm hit. Thunder. Little bats of lightning. An electrical storm in full fury. Lightning so fierce, it gouged great holes in the earth.

"Flash lightning. Then forked lightning. Chain lightning. Some colored blue."

"And formed into balls," the cowboy who spoke earlier said.

I nodded. "Lightning balls rolled on the ground. Then spark lightning. You could see it on the horns of cattle, the ears of horses, and on the brims of the men's hats. It grew so hot, the men thought they might burn up with it. Then, as the rain subsided, a fog settled over the hands, their horses, and the cattle. The air smelled of burning sulfur."

I paused to see how my audience was taking the story. I had captured them. *I can ask them for more*, I thought.

"Can you see it? Lightning playing on cattle horns? Your horse's ears? The brim of the cowboy's hats—or your own hat? Can you feel the heat? Smell that smell?"

One the cowhands rose from the bench, clutching a rolled tortilla in one hand, its end stained with chile sauce. "Sometimes," he said, "in the middle of the night, the cattle would get so restless that we would have to sing to calm them."

Remembering Papá's advice, I asked him, "What did you sing?"

His hazel eyes looked intently into mine for a moment, and then beyond me as he remembered. He removed his hat, revealing curly sand-colored hair, and in a soft and clear tenor relived his memory:

As I was walking one morning for pleasure,
I spied a cowpuncher riding along;
His hat was throwed back and his spurs were a-jinglin'
And as he approached he was singing this song:

Whoopee ti yi yo, git along, little dogies,
It's your misfortune and none of my own,
Whoopee ti yi yo, git along, little dogies,
You know that Wyoming will be your new home.

Early in the springtime we round up the dogies
Mark 'em and brand 'em and bob off their tails
Round up the horses, load up the chuck wagon
Then throw the little dogies out on the long trail.

On the second verse, his pals joined in, a bass and a baritone:

Whoopee ti yi yo, git along, little dogies,
It's your misfortune and none of my own,
Whoopee ti yi yo, git along, little dogies,
You know that Wyoming will be your new home.

The tenor resumed his solo:

Night comes on and we hold 'em on the bedground
The same little dogies that rolled on so slow
We roll up the herd and cut out the stray ones
Then roll the little dogies like never before.

Then others who had come to the stand to hear my story added their voices:

Whoopee ti yi yo, git along, little dogies,
It's your misfortune and none of my own,
Whoopee ti yi yo, git along, little dogies,
You know that Wyoming will be your new home.

I wondered if Papá had sung songs like this on the trail drives as I listened to the tenor sing the last verse:

Some boys go up the long trail for pleasure
But that's where they get it most awfully wrong
For you'll never know the trouble they give us
As we go drivin' them dogies along.

Now, all the diners, Elena, Mamá, Josefa, who had just returned, and I, too, joined in:

Whoopee ti yi yo, git along, little dogies,

It's your misfortune and none of my own,
Whoopee ti yi yo, git along, little dogies,
You know that Wyoming will be your new home.

The crowd swelled. New voices were added, more tenors, baritones and a bass, sopranos, contraltos, and some slightly off-pitch singers for a full and richly colored last chorus:

Whoopee ti yi yo, git along little dogies
It's your misfortune and none of my own
Whoopee ti yi yo, git along little dogies
You know that Wyoming will be your new home
You know that Wyoming will be your new home.

It ended with cheers, clapping, and food stomping. I pulled from under the table a sturdy wood crate we used to carry our earthenware. I stepped up onto it to elevate myself above the diners, squared my shoulders, and spread my arms. The rebozo's fringes fluttered. Those closest to me quieted. In just this side of a whisper, I began to speak. A hush rippled back over the crowd until all I could hear was a murmur. Gradually increasing the volume of my voice, I resumed my story.

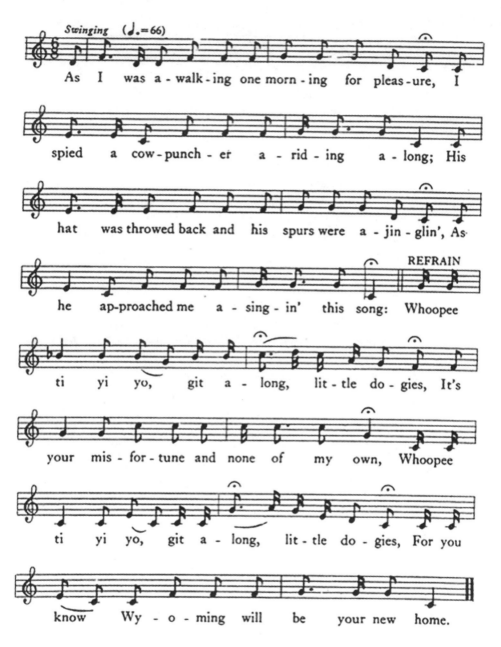

"Whoopee Ti Yi Yo, Git Along, Little Dogies"
From Lomax, John A. and Alan Lomax. Cowboy Songs and Other Frontier Ballads. London and Toronto, Ontario: Collier-Macmillan Canada LTD., The Macmillan Company, 1938. Eighteenth Printing 1969, pp. 4-6.

CHAPTER *11*

"By morning, the drive was eight miles off course. Every man worked to hold the herd, pushing all night. Flashes of lightning keep them moving. At sunup, it had gotten bitterly cold, but the rain had let up some. The crew drove the cattle back to the camping area, slogging through water the whole way. The ground was sodden, belly deep to a horse in some places. Sometimes they had to put down a mount that was too spent to go on.

"The men had not eaten or slept for two days and nights. They were famished. They were hoping for some hot grub and strong coffee when they got back to camp. But once there, they found no campfire blazing and no food cooking. The cook was huddled in the chuck wagon, trying to stay dry. The trail boss fired him on the spot.

"But that did not ease their hunger. So, Miguel fetched some dry logs from under the wagon."

"In the caboose!" one of the diners said.

"The caboose?" a lady patron asked.

"The cowhide sling under the wagon where pieces of wood are kept dry and stored for emergencies," I said. The term had been new to me, too. Papá had explained. "Several hands got a fire going with the oilcan. They pitched in to make a meal that filled every man's belly. A good night's sleep and they were ready for another day. A good thing, too. More trouble was on the horizon."

Everyone at the table seemed to lean toward me, expectation written large on their faces. On the spot, I decided to keep them guessing. "You will just have to come back tomorrow to learn what happened next," I said.

There was collective groan. "Come back tomorrow," I repeated. "The story gets better."

"I'll be back, for sure." Peter said and turned to diners nearby. "How about you?"

One of the cowboys answered for himself and his friends, "We're camped just outside town for a couple of days. We can come back." He turned to me, "Gracias, señorita. You're a good storyteller." He settled their meal costs with Elena. Before leaving, he extended his hand to drop a tip into mine. Others did the same. In minutes, I had collected eight cents in tips alone.

Peter's hand touched mine ever so gently as he added his penny to my collection. He tipped his hat, turned, and walked away. I watched his long, loose strides as his form disappeared into darkness, past the stores on the plaza's far side.

"Lupe. Lupe." Josefa had returned. Her beautiful face was radiant. She reached out to embrace me, so different from her typical reserve. "The Fashion Theater is a magical place, Lupe. There are graceful dancers, funny comedians, pretty showgirls . . . and the singers, what rich voices they have. You should see the actresses' dresses, Lupe, richly colored silk, sateen, and brocade in the latest styles from New York City. You must come to a performance. You should see Tom dance on stage. He is wonderful. Tom says he will get tickets for the whole family."

"Be careful, Josefa," I said. "You do not know this man, where he is from, what is in his past."

"I know that he makes me feel like . . ." she paused, "a grown woman, a desirable woman."

"He is a man of the world. He has seen much more than we have."

"When you get to know him better, you will understand. He is coming by later, after the show. You will see how nice he really is when you get to know him." Josefa looked at the occupied benches around our chili stand and said, "We are busy tonight. What have you been doing?" She did not wait for my answer. She turned to Elena, "Who needs to be served?"

"I do." Antonio was taking the place Peter had vacated moments earlier. Elena rushed over from the far side of the stand. She had just served a plate of fragrant chili and frijoles to the woman who had asked what a wagon's caboose was.

"What can I get for you, Antonio?" she asked.

"What is good tonight?" he asked, and I noticed something pass between them. I viewed Antonio as a friend, a big brother to take the place that my older brothers held before they had their own families to look after. Elena seemed to have a different view. I heard her call his order of enchiladas to Mamá. As soon as she moved away from him, I approached.

"Antonio," I said, and he looked directly into my eyes, his large dark ones playful.

"¿Sí?" He smiled broadly.

"You meet many men who have been on the trail in Mr. Illg's shop."

"I meet more in the cockpit," he said, referring to the cockfights where he liked to wager with friends and, especially, gamblers passing through town.

"Have you heard any trail drive corridos?"

"Cowhands sing some of the same ones. They learn them from one another. They pick them up on the trail."

"They sing in English?"

Elena placed a plate of enchiladas in front of Antonio. He acknowledged her with a smile.

"Claro. Sometimes they whistle or just hum the tune."

"There are Spanish ones?"

"Sure there are. Many."

Elena went back to where Mamá was tending the cook pots, returning to Antonio's place in moments with a chocolatero. Mama had placed a chunk of dark unsweetened chocolate in the chocolatero and added hot water.

"Well, that is what I am asking you, Antonio. Do you know one you can teach me?"

"Why? Are you planning to go on a trail drive?"

Elena was stirring several teaspoons of piloncillo into Antonio's drink and laughed at his joke. I shot her a sidelong glance. She caught my meaning and busied herself twirling a molinillo to froth the dark liquid while trying to suppress a giggle.

"I might," I said. "But right now I want a song to entertain my customers. Tonight, one of the cowhands began singing and everyone joined in. The ballad was familiar to all. I want to sing one that some may not have heard before. One I could teach them."

"That would be a new thing to do at a chili stand," Elena said.

"This is my thought, also."

"And a good one," Antonio said, holding his fork to his forehead in a salute.

"Well, do you know one you can teach me?"

Antonio nodded while chewing his enchilada. He took a sip from the cup of hot chocolate Elena placed before him, swallowed, and wiped his upper lip with the back of his hand.

"*Lo siento*," Elena said, and handed him a napkin.

"I will bring my guitar next time."

"You sing?" The voice was Tom O'Malley's.

Josefa took Tom's arm and introduced the two men.

"Only cowhand songs," Antonio said. "And only to calm the cows—or help chili queens entertain their diners." He nodded his head in my direction.

"Well, I'm always happy to meet another performer, whatever and wherever you sing." Tom said.

"Lupe tells me that you danced with her on the plaza."

Tom O'Malley smiled, he took both my hands in his. "It is good to see you again, Lupe."

I curtsied.

Josefa introduced Elena, then guided Tom to where Mamá was patting out tortillas and toasting them on the comal as quickly as Elena could pick them up for diners.

"You never curtsy for me," Antonio said.

"When you are charming, I will."

Antonio rose.

"You will be back with your guitar?"

He nodded and waved.

I glanced to the back of the stand where Josefa and Tom were animated in conversation with our mother. Mamá listened, looking tense, guarded. Then she spoke but I could not hear what she was saying. There was nothing I could do about that, anyway, so I turned away to chat with my customers.

A man in a business suit approached me. "Buenas noches, señorita, me llamo John Abramson."

I acknowledged his greeting.

"I am in town to do business with Mr. Frost. I own a sheep farm," he explained. "I was told to look for the señorita in the rebozo with the long colorful fringes if I wanted to taste the best chile sauce on the plaza. So, here I am."

"Would you like chili or enchiladas?"

"Both," he said. "*Tengo hambre esta noche.* I am hungry tonight. And café, por favor."

I called his order to Mamá. As I handed him a fork and napkin, he said, "My wife would like that rebozo."

"It is not for sale, señor."

He raised his hand in protest. "Forgive me for conveying the wrong impression. I did not think it was. But I am wondering where I might purchase one like it. I have seen many shawls in the markets and shops, but none like yours."

An idea startled me. *Why had I not thought of this before? People sell serapes and blankets on the plaza all the time. Maybe I could sell rebozos.*

"I hope that I have not offended you, señorita," he said. "It is just that it is so beautiful. It would make the perfect gift for our anniversary."

I shook my head and smiled at him. "To the contrary, señor. You have given me an idea. When will you be back in San Antonio?"

"In several months."

"Bueno. Come back here when you return." And then I made an audacious promise, "I will have rebozos for you to choose from."

"Gracias, señorita." He motioned to his plate. "And this is the best chile sauce I have ever tasted. Do you sell it, too?"

The ideas in my head swirled. "Not yet," I said, then added, "Be sure to tell your friends to visit the Pérez chili stand."

In the early morning hours, back at home, Josefa chatted on and on until dawn.

"Por favor," I pleaded. "My head is throbbing."

But Josefa was too keyed up to mind me. I was sitting with my legs dangling over the side of the bed we shared.

"You should see him dance, Lupe," she said and moved her feet in the rhythmic clogging motion that I remembered when Tom O'Malley danced with me. "And his voice—what a charming tenor. He makes you believe that he is singing only to you."

"What does Mamá think about this?"

"Oh, Lupe. You know how Mamá feels about theater people. She thinks they have questionable morals and a lifestyle that is unconventional. But Lupe, I do not see them that way at all. They are attractive people with talents to sing and dance and playact and make people laugh. I wish that I could be one of them."

Josefa could certainly hold her own with any actress in physical appearance, but she had a reserve that I did not think people like Tom O'Malley and his friends would understand.

"Tomás and his friends are so much fun!" Josefa clapped her hands.

¿Tomás?

Josefa swirled several times in place, plunked herself down beside me and took my hands in hers. Again, her face flushed. Her eyes danced. I saw in her an unbounded bliss. She told me again what she had told me before, this time with added description. She was clearly enchanted.

"Tomás introduced me to so many exciting people. I met stunning showgirls, comedians who made me laugh, dancers so light on their feet that I thought they were flying, singers who hit high notes that gave me chills, musicians who made their instruments sing. What a show they put on. The audience cheered, and at the end, kept calling for more, clapping, shouting, and stomping. I wondered what it must feel like to stand on that stage, looking out over a theater full of cheering admirers."

This was a side of Josefa I had not seen before, a side that Josefa most likely was just discovering in herself, a side laid bare by Tom O'Malley and his theater friends. I waved my sister away and fell back onto the bed, exhausted.

I awoke early, pulled on my stockings and shoes and enough clothing for a visit to the outhouse far back in the yard. Just outside the back door of our house was a washstand with a basin and a pitcher of water we filled from the rain barrel. That barrel was our source of water for washing up. A ladle hung on its rim. A towel was draped over a nail on the back wall. I poured just enough water into the basin to wash, using the bar soap Mamá bought at Mr. Orynski's drugstore on the south side of the plaza. We reserved its use for face washing. It was more expensive than the lye soap used for household cleaning and laundry, but much gentler on soft skin. I patted my face dry, wiped my hands, and went back inside to finish dressing. I jostled Josefa. She rolled onto her side, pulling the blanket over her head. I was relentless in poking and prodding her until she blinked at me groggily.

"I need to go out for a while," I told her. "You can start the chile sauce for tonight without me."

"Where are you going?"

"Later," was all I chose to say, and I headed out of the house at a brisk pace.

CHAPTER 12

anuel Lopez had been parking his mule team on the corner of South Laredo and Arsenal Streets for many years more than we had been in San Antonio. I found him straddling one of the rear animals in his six-mule team.

"Hola, Lupe. It has been a long time since I saw you."

"Buenos dias, señor Lopez."

"¿Cómo están tus padres?"

"They are well."

He dismounted and walked toward me, hand extended. I saw stiffness in his gait.

Señor Lopez parked his mule team and wagon on Laredo Street. He was astride one of the mules when I arrived to ask him to bring rebozos from Mexico for me to sell at our chili stand.
Freighters on S. Laredo Street, San Antonio, Texas, 1877, General Photograph Collection, 122: 099-0184, University of Texas at San Antonio Libraries Special Collections from the Institute of Texan Cultures.

"When I was younger, this block would be full of freighter's mule teams. *Ya no más*. Not anymore. Not since the railroad came to town. Only a few, like me, remain."

"Do you see rebozos in the Mexican markets—not just nice ones, really pretty ones?"

Señor Lopez thought for a moment. "Sí, especially in San Luis Potosí."

"Are they for sale?"

"Some are, yes. Why do you ask?"

"I would like to sell rebozos at our chili stand."

"Does your father know this?"

"Not yet. The idea just came to me last night when one of the diners asked about the rebozo I was wearing."

"And what rebozo is that?"

"A very beautiful silk one, vermillion and indigo, and woven into a striped pattern with long, intricately knotted fringes."

"You are not looking for everyday rebozos then."

"No, señor. I want special ones. But they do not need to be silk. They can be cotton or wool, so long as the thread is fine, the pattern colorful, and the fringes long and distinctive."

"Still, they will not be cheap. One rebozo like that could cost me as much as two, three, or four dollars. I would need to charge you at least a third more to cover my time and travel. They would cost you anywhere from about three to five and thirty—each."

I had anticipated the costs, based on what I knew shawls sold for in the local stores and the range of prices in catalogues.

"How many will you need?"

"I would like to order five."

I saw the look in señor Lopez's eyes change. *Él no cree que tenga el dinero. He does not believe that I have the money.* He was right.

"I can sell rebozos at a good profit," I said. I did not know that. It was my hope. Señor Lopez was an astute businessman. He probably sensed my bluff. Papá had told me to take charge. So I told him, with as much confidence as I could muster, "I will pay you in full and in cash after I sell the rebozos."

He shook his head. "The railroad has taken much of my business. My profits are not what they once were, and I still have to support my family, feed my animals, keep my wagon in good repair, and stock provisions for my long trips into Mexico and back."

"Señor Lopez, if you supply me with beautiful robozos, I know that I can sell them at a good profit. If I do well, I will reorder and increase the number over time."

A long moment of silence followed. It seemed like he would never speak. And then he said, "I must have payment on delivery—the full amount."

I felt his determination and knew that he would not bargain further. I had no idea where I would get the money, but I accepted his terms. "Bueno." I offered my hand in agreement. "When do you think you can deliver?"

"In two months' time."

On the walk home, I grappled with the question of how I could raise fifteen to twenty-six and fifty—in only sixty days. That night I confided in Elena.

"How much have you saved from tips?" she asked.

"So far this week, *diez centavos*. Ten cents—to add to the dollar and fifty I already had."

"You can have my five."

"I am not asking for your money, Elena. I will not be able to pay you back right away."

"I am *giving* you the money, Lupe. You do not need to pay it back. You are my friend and I want to help you. You dream big, Lupe. I do not know how to do that. But I can help you chase your dream." Elena untied a knot at the end of her handkerchief, gathered the five pennies, and handed them to me.

I felt a wellspring of gratitude. Five cents would not add much to the total fund, but Elena's unselfish and considerate gesture touched me. I wrapped my arms around her and held her tight. Our friendship was lop-sided. Elena was the giver, I, the taker. That bothered me, but it seemed to be just the way things were between us. I brushed aside the quandary with the thought that one day I would repay Elena for her generosity. Now, I needed what others could give.

"Where will you get the rest of the money?"

"No sé, Elena. I have to think about that."

"Maybe from Antonio? He has a good paying job and he always seems to have money."

I hugged her. "You have good ideas, Elena."

The next time Antonio came to the chili stand, he arrived with his guitar slung over his shoulder. The colorfully woven strap crossed his chest like a bandoleer.

"You have a corrido for me?"

"There is one I have heard many times. It is called 'Kiansis.'" He shifted the guitar forward. The finish on the wood beneath the sound hole where a pick guard should have been was badly scared. Scraggly string ends protruded from the tuners. The instrument looked old, tired. But when Antonio worked his fingers along the frets and rhythmically strummed its strings, the old body sang.

Antonio started to hum the first bar. *"Kian-sis con una grande . . . "* he started, paused, and began again, still sotto voce. Then, in his full, clear tenor, he sang the entire song, word for word:

From Paredes, Américo. A Texas-Mexican Cancionero: Folksongs of the Lower Border. Urbana-Champaign, Ill.: University of Illinois Press, 1976. pp. 53-54.

"Kiansis"
Cuando salimos pa' Kiansis
con una grande partida
¡ah, qué camino tan largo!
no contaba con mi vida.

Nos decía el caporal,
como queriendo llorar:
—Allá va la novillada,
no me la dejen pasar.—

¡Ah, qué caballo tan bueno!
todo se le iba en correr,

¡y, ah, qué fuerte aguacerazo!
no contaba yo en volver.

Unos pedían cigarro,
otros pedían que comer,
y el caporal nos decía:
—Sea por Dios, qué hemos de hacer.—

En el charco de Palomas
se cortó un novillo bragado,
y el caporal lo lazó
en su caballo melado.

Avísenle al caporal
que un vaquero se mató,
en las trancas del corral
nomás la cuera dejó.

Llegamos al Río Salado
y nos tiramos a nado,
decía un americano:
—Esos hombes ya se ahogaron.—

Pues qué pensaría ese hombre
que venimos a esp'rimentar,
si somos del Río Grande,
de los buenos pa'nadar.

Y le dimos vista a Kiansis,
y nos dice el caporal:
—Ora sí somos de vida,
ya vamos a hacer corral.—

Y de vuelta en San Antonio
compramos buenos sombreros,
y aquí se acaban cantando
versos de los aventureros.

"Teach it to me."

The following Sunday afternoon, Antonio came to dinner at my house with his guitar, and afterwards, in our yard, he schooled me in the song, verse by verse. My memory was strong. It did not take long to learn the lyrics. My young nieces and nephews did even better. They were singing it by heart after only a couple of hearings. The straightforward, repetitive melody line made it easy. I was ready to weave the song into my story the next week. I did on Wednesday.

As soon as four or five customers had assembled and Elena had taken orders, I clapped my hands to get their attention.

"I have another story, if you would be pleased to hear it."

"What about?" one man asked.

"Another adventure of Miguel Martinez on the range."

Heads nodded. A few clapped their interest.

I held out my rebozo-covered arms and began:

"One year on the cattle trail, the trail boss told his crew of Kineños, vaqueros from the King ranch. 'We are taking the river route.'"

"Hope it weren't a flood year," one man chuckled. The others hushed him.

"They crossed the San Antonio; the Guadalupe near Gonzales; the San Marcos; the Colorado at Austin; the Brazos and Lampasas; the Pease at Vernon; the Red River South Fork at Donner, Oklahoma; the Cimarron; the Wichita; and the Arkansas. There were no bridges. They had to ford every river. The vaqueros laughed, 'We are from the Río Bravo. We are good swimmers,' they said.

"They needed to be when the rivers were on a rampage. Crossing one in midstream, Miguel was swept off his horse. He sank straight down to the bottom. He fought his way to the surface. His horse swam toward shore. He struck out in the same direction. But the current was too strong and he drifted downstream several hundred yards. A friend started toward him on his horse. As he passed by, Jesse grabbed onto the horse's tail. But they all got caught in a wide eddy that carried them under a bluff where they could not land. They had to drift downstream until the eddy changed, then swim to the opposite side of the river where Miguel's horse had come ashore. Soaked, Miguel stripped off his wet clothes, hung them on tree limbs to dry, and stark naked, joined the other men who were moving cattle across the river."

I noticed sheepish grins on a couple of men who had come to listen to my story and saw a blush rise on the face of a young woman sitting at the table. I thought I needed to settle the issue right away.

"Miguel was not naked the whole of the two days it took to get the herd safely across. He donned his wrinkled clothes as soon as they were dry enough to wear."

By now the stand was filling with customers, and Josefa, Elena, and Mamá were struggling to meet the demand. I wanted to help them serve, but diners would be impatient for their food if I did not hold their attention with my story. I continued:

"One horse refused to cross. They tried to get him to swim, but he would turn on his side, curl his tail between his legs, and float back to the bank." I held out my hand, palm down, giving it a quarter turn while locking my thumb between my fisted fingers to imitate the animal's behavior. "He was a fine-looking red roan—not a horse to lose. They spent another day building a raft to ferry him and a few other reluctant swimmers across. You can imagine how famished the men were, having had nothing to eat until the work was done. What they would have given for a plate of our enchiladas, a bowl of our chili, or our frijoles and fresh tortillas!" I paused to let them realize how lucky they were as Elena set their savory meals before them.

"Thunderstorms were heavy in wet years, this being one of them. The same night they had arrived safely on the far bank, a big one came up. It was dreadful. Horses put their heads between their legs and moaned. Cattle stampeded. Stomping hooves and rattling horns added to the thunderous din. It took three more days to round up the strays and head them north to Kansas.

"To soothe the animals, and maybe to calm their own nerves, the vaqueros sang."

Softly, I whistled the tune, and then sang the first verse of "Kiansis" the way Antonio had taught me. A passerby stopped to add his voice to the second verse. I fluttered the fringes of my rebozo with the beat. And to my surprise and delight, as I began the third verse, most at the table joined in, humming or whistling the tune as we sang the lyrics. Antonio arrived just in time to harmonize, and the volume of voices swelled as our music attracted newcomers. They quickly picked up the melody. Hands clapped out the rhythm. Feet marked the accents.

When the song was done, a woman seated on the bench to my right stood up to speak, "Señorita, I am from St. Louis. The melody is pretty, but I do not know what you are saying."

"English words do not fit the melody well," I told her. "But I can tell you what they mean.

"'Kiansis' is sung by a vaquero on a long and hard trail drive. He tells us about moving a large herd of cattle to Kansas. During the drive, a thunderstorm hits. The men are hungry and short on supplies. But the trail boss keeps them going.

"At one point, an angry steer gets loose and the trail boss chases and lassoes him.

"At another place, one of the vaqueros gets killed. They leave his jacket hanging on a rail post, marking the spot.

"The vaqueros swim their horses and the herd across the Salado River. An American thinks they might drown. But the vaqueros are from the Río Grande. They know how to swim. They get the cattle to Kansas. And, when they return to San Antonio, the men buy new hats with their earnings."

"Thank you," the woman said. "Will you sing it again?"

We did and the diners clamored for a third time, and a fourth. The rebozo's fringes seemed to flutter all on their own. I looked up to see Peter smiling at me.

"You have many talents, señorita Pérez. You never cease to amaze me."

His eyes were soft, his expression, sincere.

"Gracias." I felt my face grow warm.

"Mr. Kotula offered me the use of his buggy on Sunday afternoon. Would you permit me to take you to San Pedro Park?"

My heart was beating furiously now. I had to take a deep breath before answering. "I would very much like that. But you will have to ask my Papá if he will allow it."

"I would not have approached you without his permission."

"And he agreed?"

Peter nodded. "Provided you wish to join me."

"I would like to, very much. But we may not go off alone. Another member of the family must accompany us."

"Yes, of course."

"When will you come for us?"

"Sunday. At three o'clock." He hesitated. His eyes clouded. "I just thought of something. There is a small problem."

"¿Qué?"

"The buggy seats only two."

CHAPTER *13*

"I will go with you and Mr. Meyer on Sunday," Josefa said as we were preparing for another night on the plaza.

"Papá has asked you?"

Josefa nodded. "Mamá cannot. The house will be full of family on Sunday afternoon. Papá says we can take the trolley. He will pay my fare. I am happy to do this for you, little sister."

Soon after we got set up, Josefa disappeared. I had too much on my mind to worry about her continuing liaisons with Tom O'Malley. Our stand was attracting more customers. I was grateful to Elena for helping in Josefa's absence. I did not expect her to work for nothing. Her father sold candy. Her mother was a cleaning woman. Now out of school, Elena was expected to contribute to her family's income. Working all night at a chili stand made her daytime labor harder. She could do odd jobs like laundry and mending, but she needed time to sleep between shifts. Our income was not yet strong enough to pay her a salary. Elena agreed to work for tips only, not much for the long, late hours we asked of her. Her help was much needed, but it made another problem. The only solution was to increase profits—substantially and soon.

Peter arrived earlier than usual.

"I can't stay long this evening," he told me. "I came to ask about Sunday."

"Josefa will accompany us. Papá says we must travel together. He suggests we take the trolley."

Peter's expression remained dispassionate. I found it difficult sometimes to read him. The men I had grown up with were much more expressive in word and manner.

"All right." He paused. His brow furrowed ever so slightly. I studied his face and caught the hint of a nod. "I will tell Mr. Kotula about the change in plans. Perhaps we can use the buggy another time. I will come for you at three o'clock," he said. "Until Sunday, then. Good evening, señorita Pérez." He tipped his hat and left.

Sunday Mass at San Fernando seemed unusually long. And afterward, time dragged on with the gossipy conversations among my parents and friends on Main Plaza. When we finally got home, our extended family dinner was delayed because one of my sisters was late. Her toddler had been slow to rise that morning. San Fernando's bells chimed one o'clock before we were all at table. They signaled half past two before the table had been cleared. Thankfully, Mamá excused me from the cleanup. I left it to my sisters and sisters-in-law to wash, dry, and stack the dishes on the table in readiness for the next meal.

I wished I had something special to wear, but I had only the skirts and bodices that Josefa and I shared. The one in the best condition was dark blue. The skirt hem and the bodice collar and cuffs were threadbare, but we did our best to keep them clean and they fitted me well. I looked down at the skirt, reaching behind to smooth its folds over my soft bustle. *Too dark for a sunny June day. It needs some color. The rebozo. I need to wear the rebozo.*

I ran into the yard where Mamá was rolling a ball to one of her grandchildren.

"*Mamá, ¿puedo llevar el rebozo de seda?* Mamá, may I wear the silk rebozo?"

She regarded me seriously. "*Solo si te gusta mucho este joven.* Only if you like this young man very much. Do not forget its magic."

"Sí, Mamá."

"You know, Lupe, that Peter Meyer is different from us. "

"He is not so different from me, Mamá. He shares some of the same dreams."

"Do not get your hopes too high."

"What if he likes me as much as I like him?"

"Well . . . perhaps. He seems like a fine young man."

"Then, I may wear the rebozo?"

"Sí, Lupita. Just be careful not to lose your heart too quickly."

I spun on my heels and ran inside to get the treasured garment from the trunk. I draped it over my shoulders, winding each end around my forearms so that the fringes fluttered with the motion of my hands and arms. I felt better—colorful, pretty, happy, and ready for my first outing with Peter Meyer.

He arrived at exactly three o'clock, just as he had promised. His shirt was bright white, its collar well starched. His suit looked pressed, his shoes shined, and the nap on his bowler had been brushed all in one direction. Peter was not handsome in the way Tom O'Malley was, but I thought him to be the finest-looking man I had ever known.

The family hushed. All, even the little children, watched as Peter presented a small burlap sack of flower seeds to Mamá and a pouch of tobacco to Papá. He and Papá shook hands as he thanked both for the visit we were about to have. He introduced himself to all the men and they presented their wives. Everyone seemed awkward, except for the little ones. I could not swallow the lump in my throat. When the formalities were done, Peter offered one arm to me, the other to Josefa. At the front door, he stepped aside for each of us to pass through onto Laredo Street. He joined us and offered a steady arm to Josefa and to me.

"The trolley travels down Houston from Alamo Plaza. It turns north on Acequia, then turns onto Romano on its way to San Pedro Avenue," he told us. "The driver will stop for ladies. The turn from Houston to Acequia usually slows the mule anyway. We should be able to board there."

We walked the familiar several blocks along Laredo to Dolorosa, where daily we turned east on Caballo, toward Military Plaza. Peter guided us northbound along the side of the plaza behind San Fernando Cathedral and past the nightly location of our chili stand. I had to hasten to keep up with his long strides. Josefa, too. We were both much shorter than he and could not match his pace, taking two steps to his one. It was difficult to make conversation. After a failed attempt to breathlessly comment on the glorious warm and sunny afternoon, I stopped trying. Peter was clearly in a hurry.

"I want to catch the very next trolley," he said. "It would be a shame to spend our time waiting for transport."

We crossed West Commerce. At Houston Street, we turned north.

When we got to the intersection of Acequia and Houston Streets and could see the tracks, Peter relaxed. "There, look up Houston."

Coming toward us was a mule-drawn trolley car. The driver sat in front and outside of a small open car. Several passengers occupied the crosswise

Peter, Josefa, and I walked past the rear of San Fernando Cathedral on Military Plaza to Houston where we caught the trolley for San Pedro Springs Park.
Detail of Bird's Eye View of San Antonio, 1886, by Augustus Koch Courtesy of the Witte Museum, San Antonio, Texas.

bench seats but there was still room for us. Most of the park visitors this Sunday afternoon had already reached their destination. We were latecomers.

Peter hailed the trolley and it gradually slowed.

The driver reined in the mule. But instead of halting between the rails, the animal veered right, pulling the car off the track. The trolley came to a disabled halt.

"Damn mule," I heard the driver swear under his breath. "Pardon me, ladies," he added quickly. "Gentlemen, please help the ladies off," he called back to the passengers. "Then, give a hand to get us back on track."

Peter removed his jacket and hat and handed them to me, motioning us to move back, away from the car. The other men removed their jackets as well, leaving them with the women or draped over a car bench. The driver unhitched the mule. Peter and two other men took hold of the running board on the derailed side of the trolley. Three men did the same on the other side. At the driver's signal, the men on one side lifted and pushed while those on the other pulled and steadied. The car yielded, but one man lost his hold and it dropped back off the track. Again, the men leaned into the task. This time the little car moved. The men on Peter's side pushed and those on the far side pulled, landing the car on its tracks. The driver hitched the mule back into position and waved us on board.

The women passengers resumed their places, chatting merrily about the incident. They were wearing white dresses and straw hats, some set at a fashionable angle. The men swung up on seats beside them. I felt a bit shabby by comparison. I smiled at one woman, but she looked away. An-

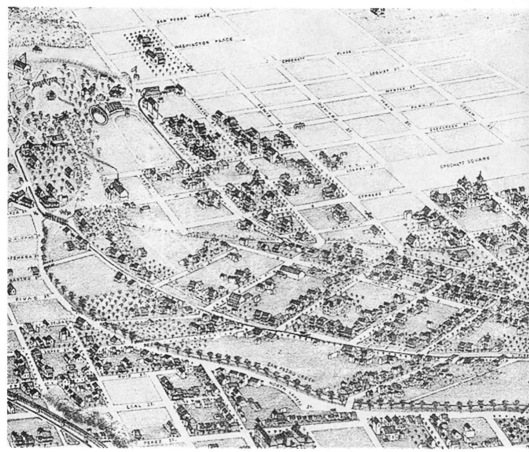

The mule-drawn trolley to San Pedro Springs Park traveled on tracks that ran alongside a racetrack and into a carriage house. This detail of Mr. Koch's bird's eye view of San Antonio shows the park in the upper left hand corner. You can see the lake with its island and footbridge where we stopped to look into the crystal clear water and see colorful fish in its depths. Visits to San Pedro Springs Park with Peter are some of my fondest memories of our times together.
Detail of northwest section of Bird's Eye View of San Antonio, 1886, by Augustus Koch. Courtesy of the Witte Museum, San Antonio, Texas.

other eyed my silk rebozo, I could not decide if with approval, interest, or disdain. She did not look directly at me.

Peter helped Josefa and me step onto the running board and into the car, motioning us to take seats on a vacant section of bench.

Satisfied that we were all in place, the driver shook the reins and we were northbound, soon leaving behind the more populous area of the city. The park was only a mile from Main Plaza, but it seemed to me that in that short distance the air felt cooler. More trees lined the street and fewer residences were visible. It grew quieter. The click-clack of the car on the rails beat a rhythmic accompaniment to bird song. Shortly after passing a large oval racetrack, the trolley pulled into a carriage house where fresh mules awaited their turn. The ride had taken about half an hour, lengthened by the derailing. We could have walked the distance in less time, especially at Peter's pace. But that would not have been as enjoyable.

Peter helped me, then Josefa, from the car. The driver spoke to him and he handed the man our fares.

"Did Mr. Meyer just pay for me?" Josefa asked me.

"I think so."

When he returned to us, Josefa offered him the six-and-a-half-cent fare. He demurred. "You are my guest, too."

Peter offered an arm to each of us and guided us through the San Pedro Springs Park portal, just across from the carriage house. We walked past a grassy knoll and the dance pavilion. Overhanging trees lined the banks of a large, clear lake. Our path crossed a wooden footbridge across the lake. I had been to San Pedro Springs Park before, for *Diez y Seis*, Mexican Independence Day, when we set up our chili stand for the evening's celebration. In daylight, I saw so much more.

From the bridge, many springs bubbled up, feeding the lake. Here were the headsprings of San Pedro Creek. The water was crystal clear. Its scent was fresh, unspoiled by refuse and manure like the flow of creek water that meandered through town. I saw catfish and trout in the lake's depths. I watched them dart among the lakebed ferns, and pointed out brilliantly colored perch to Peter and Josefa. Swans and ducks glided on the lake's glistening surface.

"How did the springs form?" I asked Peter.

"In early geologic time, earthquakes caused faults in the rocks. Underground springs bubble up from limestone under hydrostatic pressure."

"But how did the water get down there?"

"When it rains, surface water runs over the fractures and crevices in the rock. There are many of them along the Balcones Fault. See the dimples and holes in surface rocks? They were formed by dripping water on the porous limestone. The water drips through the limestone into large holes in the ground, where it accumulates. Large caves are underground. One was found recently to contain human skeletal remains, arrowheads, and some pottery shards."

"How do you know this?"

Peter smiled. "I like to read."

We continued our leisurely stroll, at a pace much more comfortable

Peter, Josefa, and I took this footbridge across the lake at San Pedro Springs Park. It was from the bridge that I peered into the clear lake to watch colorful fish in its depths. We walked along the tree-lined path. *Path Through Trees, San Pedro Park, San Antonio, Texas, 1880-1889. General Photograph Collection, 136: 101-0074, University of Texas at San Antonio Special Collections from the Institute of Texan Cultures.*

for me than our hurried walk to catch the trolley. We followed the paths around six smaller lakes. Families sat on benches at picnic tables in little retreats, colorful with tropical flowers. Soft breezes swayed the long, broad leaves of banana trees. Some picnickers were seated on thick blankets they had spread on the ground. Children scampered about. An energetic game of ring-around-the-rosy was underway when we passed.

"Oh, listen," I said. "A band is playing."

"Let's go closer." Peter led us to the eastern lakeshore where a pecan grove shaded tables and benches near a bandstand. A German beer garden and the dance pavilion were filled with couples and families drinking beer, dancing, and listening to lively polkas and lilting waltzes played by the San Pedro Springs Orchestra.

Peter seated us at an unclaimed table. "Would you like a beer?" He looked to each of us for response.

I nodded. But Josefa declined. "You enjoy your drinks together," she said. "I am going to walk through the flower gardens while you visit. I will join you here later."

Peter left to get us beer. "Gracias, Josefa," I said. The tilt of her smile let me know that she was not doing this for me alone. *She must have arranged to meet Tom O'Malley here.*

People seated at tables around me appeared refined in dress and manner. Their clothing murmured quality and newness. Women were wearing the very latest fashions, like those worn by the young ladies on the trolley. They held parasols to shield their fair skin from the sun. Some were speaking German. I felt out of place, uncomfortable—until Peter returned. He set before me a mug of amber liquid capped with milk-white foam. Tiny bubbles rose from the bottom of the mug, making the liquid sparkle. I did not touch it right away. Peter took a sip of his and smiled his approval. He nodded to my glass. "Drink while it is cold."

I gingerly raised the cool mug to my lips, took a very small sip, and felt the soft foam and the beer's tingle against my upper lip. One sip and the amber brew filled my mouth with strong flavor. A few more and I found my voice.

"It was very nice of Mr. Kotula to offer you his horse and buggy. I am sorry that we could not use it."

"He said that we had done well in the store over the past month. Loan of his buggy was a bonus. The trolley ride was enjoyable, though. My only regret is that I could not transport you from your front door. Still, I would have had the buggy only until about six o'clock or so. Our visit here would have been brief. The trolley operates until midnight. With longer springtime days, we can relax here awhile, and I can still make sure you return home before dark." Peter's eyes scanned the park. He turned to give me a wistful smile. "I wish we could be here when the gas lamps flicker their light across the water. It is a scene from the *Arabian Nights*. It would suit you."

"In what way?"

"You are a modern-day Scheherazade at your chili stand, are you not?"

I laughed. I had not thought of myself in that way. But I liked the comparison and gladly embraced it. "Why yes, I guess I am—or at least I am trying to be."

"I would venture to say that you are doing very well in that role, señorita Pérez. I enjoy your stories and you always make me want to return for more."

"I hope that you will feel comfortable calling me by my given name, a nickname at that."

"Of course, if you will do the same. But I do not have a nickname."

"I must admit that I think of you as Peter." It was the first time I had spoken his name to him and doing so gave me a start.

"One day, Lupe," Peter said, as if calling me by my given name was the most natural thing in the world, "I will have a horse and buggy of my own to use whenever I wish for as long as I want. When I have my store."

"When do you think that will be?"

"It will take some years yet. There's a lot to learn just to start a business. I'll need some capital. Of course, making it profitable is another matter altogether."

"How did Mr. Kotula make his business grow?"

"That's what I'm learning. I know that he keeps very precise records of his costs, sales, and profits. He says it is important to keep in stock those wares your customers buy regularly, and to maintain reasonable prices. Gradually, you add new items, little by little, those that customers request and those they may learn to need and want."

"Why do you want a store of your own?"

"I'd like to have a family and a nice house and be somebody in this town. It takes money to do that, enough to support a wife, raise children, enlarge your business, and have some to donate for places like this park. One day I might have a park or a place named for me."

"How will you get started?"

"I'll have to get a loan."

"How?"

"I've opened an account with Traders National Bank. In time, after I have enough saved to serve as collateral, with Mr. Kotula as a reference, I'll apply for a loan to fund my initial store and inventory."

"I have dreams, too."

"Will you share them with me?"

"I want to make my family's chili stand the place people visiting the plaza come to first. I want loyal customers. I would like to make a nice profit each week."

"Maybe open your own café?"

"Oh, I do not want to set my goals too high."

"Why not?"

"Where would I get the money? I am a young woman. I cannot get a loan from a bank."

"Perhaps you could find someone who'll help you." He looked away, toward the lake. A breeze rippled the leaves on the overhanging trees. I took another sip of my beer and waited for him to speak. Peter turned toward me, his eyes searching my face. "I . . . I would like someone—a wife who understands—to share my hopes, my aspirations, and to help me realize them."

My heart leapt in my chest. *I would like to be that woman*, I thought, but only nodded my understanding.

Peter raised his beer mug in an unspoken toast. I raised my mug and we clinked and drank. His eyes looked intently into mine over the rim of his almost-empty mug. In this instant, the music, the people, the chatter, all faded away. I was aware only of Peter's presence and my strong desire to be with him, to let no one else into our world.

"See who is here!"

Josefa shattered my moment.

Tom O'Malley's handsome grin was intrusive. Attention getting. Dominating. He made a sweeping bow to me and shook Peter's hand.

"Come along, Josefa," he said. "The band is playing. It's dance time."

We watched as the two joined the dancers, soon becoming the center of attention. Other couples formed a circle around the perimeter of the dance pavilion. Josefa and Tom were now the only dancers in the center of the floor and the focus of foot-stomping, hand-clapping attention. I, too, could not take my eyes off their beauty in motion.

"Your sister is courting danger, Lupe. Mr. O'Malley is a charming itinerant. I think that you know that."

"I do."

He took both my hands in his. "You must warn her."

CHAPTER 14

"*Three thousand head of cattle, four hundred horses, one hundred saddle horses, fifteen men in all, and only three six-shooters in the outfit," I began my story. Peter had come to hear me. So had nine others now seated around our tables. Elena was serving. Mamá was patting out and grilling tortillas. Josefa had once again disappeared.

"They had reached the Comanche reservation. The chief wanted horses and provisions as a toll to pass through and graze the cattle. When it was discovered that he spoke Spanish, Miguel was appointed to negotiate."

I repositioned the rebozo, throwing its right end over my left shoulder with a flourish while Elena took the orders of two new customers.

"Did he go alone?" one of them asked.

I nodded. "Sí. A group of mounted Comanches escorted Miguel several miles to a tepee deep in the interior of the reservation. Inside, he found a frail and elderly chief seated at the center of a circle of young braves. The two began a conversation about their experiences on the open range. The men passed the pipe around while the chief reminisced about every trail he had traversed from Laredo to El Paso. He remembered the names of all the rivers he had crossed—the Nueces, Llano, Devils, Guadalupe, Pecos, Concho, and Colorado—and all the creeks in between. He showed Miguel some burrs he had taken from cypress trees at the head of the Guadalupe River. Miguel complimented him on his knowledge of the land and its waterways.

"Then Miguel made the offer he had been authorized to make. They would give one horse and provisions for permission to pass through the reservation. 'You must pay with two beeves, a mare, and a yearling colt,' the chief countered. 'My son,' the chief put his hand on the shoulder of a young man seated to his right, 'will select them from your herds.'"

"That was a fair toll," a customer said, then bit into his frijole-laden tortilla.

"Truly. Miguel thought so, too. He had been authorized to give more if necessary." I paused a brief moment and added, "But the best was yet to come."

I scanned my audience. Twelve pair of expectant eyes trained on me. I wondered if they could guess what came next. I paused again, giving them time to speculate.

"Miguel returned to camp with the chief's son and his party of braves. He explained the deal he had struck to the trail boss. The cook was told to place on the ground a sack each of flour, sugar, and coffee, a side of bacon, several bags of prunes and beans, and canned goods from the chuck wagon. The braves gathered these items and the boss allowed them to cut two cows from the herd. Miguel took the chief's son to the makeshift corrals the men had made with rope strung around tree trunks. The brave took his time. 'He was a good judge of horseflesh,' Miguel later told the trail boss. 'He selected a pinto filly and a yearling colt, both well-muscled, with glossy coats and healthy manes and tails.'

"The Indians left with their toll and bid them farewell."

"Bet that was not the last they saw of them," a cowboy guessed, finishing his meal. He paid Elena but did not leave his seat. I had to move the story along. People were waiting for seats at our stand.

"Early the next morning, as the crew headed the herd out of the bedding grounds northbound, twenty braves arrived on beautiful horses, brushed to gleaming, their long manes and tails combed to fullness. The hands expected an attack. But the braves signaled that they had come to assist. They helped swim the cattle across the swollen river. Several of the men's horses bogged in quicksand and had to be dug out. The braves helped rescue them. And then, after all the horses and cattle were safely across, the braves treated the crew to a riding exhibition."

"The Comanche I seen rode better 'n me," a cowboy said, "and I thought I was one of the best."

"It was just as our friend here said. Riding full gallop, bareback, the braves slid to one side of the horse, hanging on by a foot hooked over the horse's rump and grasping a fistful of mane. They rode all over the horses' backs, off on one side, standing up, lying down, and even shooting arrows that hit their mark at full gallop.

"One brave challenged Miguel to lasso him. After several taunts, Miguel mounted his fastest mustang, readied his lasso, and waited. The brave passed at racing speed, lying flat on his horse. Miguel signaled his mount to follow, took aim, and threw his rope. It encircled both horse and rider. The Indian's horse shied around a tree and all four hit the ground hard when the rope tightened. Up first, Miguel ran to the brave, fearing him badly injured. But neither horse nor man was hurt. The tightly drawn rope had knocked the wind out of the Comanche and Miguel offered apologies, thinking he would be offended. But when the brave could breathe again, he just laughed and the men parted on good terms.

"The trail drive resumed without further incident—until they met Quanah Parker." I paused to let that sink in. "But that is another story for another time."

I spread my arms in response to applause, fluttering the fringes of my rebozo. I curtsied in thanks for the tips that outstretched hands placed in my palms or dropped on the table. Peter leaned toward me to whisper, "Another interesting one, señorita Scheherazade. I will return for the next installment."

"Enjoyed that. Very interesting. You are a good storyteller," diners commented as they vacated their seats to others. I would retell my story after new diners placed their orders.

José helped Elena clear the table of used plates, cups, and utensils. "Is that a story you heard from Papá?" he asked me.

"Miguel *is* Papá."

My little brother stopped in front of me, his hands full of dirty dishes. "The cattle drive is where I should be, not at a chili stand."

"It is a life for young men without attachments and with a desire for adventure," a middle aged man said to José. He was wearing a fine-quality gray felt hat, its crown made distinctive with two even creases; a white in-town shirt; and finely tooled leather chaps.

"I want to be under the stars, on horseback, singing to the cattle at night, and living close to the land."

"My name is Samuel Bishop. I'm a trail boss," the man said, and held his hand out to José.

My little brother put down the plates he was carrying, wiped his hands on a towel tucked in his belt, and grasped the older man's hand. Right there in front of me, he appeared to grow from a boy into a man.

"I am called José Pérez," he said.

Mr. Bishop nodded. "I have several hundred head bedded down for the night with my crew a few miles outside of town. When we got here from Laredo, a couple of my crew took off. I'm looking for good hands to replace them. Do you have experience with horses and cattle?"

"I used to help the vaqueros on the King Ranch with cattle roundups."

Mr. Bishop raised his eyebrows and rubbed the stubble on his chin. "How old are you?"

"Sixteen."

I glared at José and addressed Mr. Bishop. "He is fifteen."

José blushed. "My birthday is soon."

"That so?" the trail boss said.

José nodded. "I can ride better than many older men. I am strong and I have stamina." He paused, took a deep breath, looked squarely at Mr. Bishop, and added, "I was born on the King Ranch. I rode before I walked. My father was Captain King's head wrangler. He taught me to be a *jinete*—a skilled horseman. I can handle any horse you give me. I have gentled and trained mustangs straight from the wild herds. I have been on roundups to bring in hundreds of unbroken horses. I yearn for the saddle, for the open country. I hate the city."

"I like you, young man. You appear to have admirable qualities." He paused, looking intently at José. "Tell me, why did you leave the King Ranch—a place that offers a future of the type you say you want for yourself?"

"If it had been up to me, I would not have left. My father decided to come here after an accident crippled him. I do not know why. Captain King held him in high regard."

I wondered about that, too. Why had Papá taken us away from our friends, the work he loved, and our home? We were not doing as well in San Antonio. Papá avoided talking about it.

"I can start you at twelve dollars a month, the wages I pay jinetes."

What José said next surprised me. "I can make a dollar a day as a day laborer."

"But you don't get work every day."

"In good months, I can get work for fifteen or more days."

"And some months you get none."

"Maybe less, but never none."

"Then why are you working here?"

"To help my family."

"You'd do better with the guaranteed monthly wages I offer."

"I know from the cowboys who eat at our stand that some can make between twenty and fifty dollars a month."

"If they're experienced, perhaps."

"I think if they are American, they earn more than the skilled and experienced Mexicans."

I had thought of José as my baby brother, an innocent boy, but no more.

Mr. Bishop furrowed his brow. He was silent for a long moment. "I have no proof that you can do what you say."

"Let me show you, then. Give me your wildest horse and in a few days, it will be broke to saddle and rider."

"I don't have time for that. I can't hold the cattle or my men on the bedding grounds for much longer. We must be moving on."

"Give me a chance. I will not disappoint you."

"You have gumption, young man. Here's my offer. I can start you at twelve dollars with the promise of an increase to fourteen after you prove yourself. If you are an asset on your first drive, I would increase your monthly pay to sixteen, guaranteed, work or play, provided you contract for a year."

"That is fair." José's face lit up in a smile I rarely saw. Mr. Bishop had touched a passion in him that I had not fully understood. He held out his hand, but Mr. Bishop did not take it.

"Before we make a deal," Mr. Bishop said, "I must talk to your father. Will you arrange that?"

"Tomorrow afternoon. Can you be here between four and five o'clock? That is when Papá and I set up the chili stand."

"I'd planned to stay two days to find a few good hands. Until tomorrow, then." The trail boss tipped his fine hat and left.

"*Regatea bien*, José," I said. "You bargain well. Even so, it will not come to pass. I hope you will not be too disappointed. Papá will never approve."

José just grinned and pushed passed me, carrying dishes to the washbasin.

True to his word, Samuel Bishop arrived while we were setting up the chili stand the next afternoon. I watched surreptitiously as Elena and I placed cloths, lanterns, and earthenware on the tables. The two approached Papá, who was expecting them. They spoke in hushed tones, clearly not wanting others to know their business, so I could not hear them. After a lengthy conversation, they shook hands. Then I saw Mr. Bishop and José walk away together. A little more than an hour later, by the church chimes, they returned, not on foot.

The horses I usually saw on the plaza pulled produce and hay wagons that were parked there during the day. I rarely saw men bring their mounts onto the plaza at night. Most boarded them at one of the livery stables nearby, the place where Mr. Bishop had probably left his horse when he came into town. The trail boss was astride a large, well-groomed palomino. José's was smaller and scruffy, but it was a well-muscled blue roan. I guessed it to be a mustang colt. A little serious grooming and it would be quite handsome.

They dismounted. Mr. Bishop called a boy who was with a farming family packing their wagon for the ride home. He dropped some coins into the boy's palm and handed him the reins to the palomino. Without being told, José handed over the reins to the roan. He and the boy knew one another from earlier days. But now, both understood that Jose´s status had changed and the boy almost bowed to him. José was wearing new clothes and polished boots. He strode toward Mamá with a gait I guessed was influenced by both the boots and his newfound self-confidence. He folded Mamá in his arms. She held him close for a long moment. He pulled away from her embrace to shake Papá's hand. Papá patted him on the back and walked with him toward me. I saw Mamá brush the tips of her fingers under her eyes.

"Mr. Bishop has bought a horse with saddle, tack, a suit of clothes, and boots for me." José's words were breathy with excitement. He motioned to the roan. "I will pay from my salary. Then the horse and tack will be my own."

I knew how much that meant to him. We had very little that any of us could call our personal possessions. To have an able horse! Well, that offered independence and mobility.

"I will see you again, Lupita. Maybe on the way back from Kansas. Before we start another drive. This is my dream come true." José flashed a grin that lit up his face. His eyes were bright.

"Do you have everything you need?"

He nodded. "Mr. Bishop outfitted me completely."

"Be careful, José."

"I know what I am doing, Lupita."

"Adiós."

With that, he gave me a hug and he and Papá headed back to where Mr. Bishop was waiting with the horses. The two mounted and headed west. I stared at my brother's receding back and the even rhythm of the roan's rump. Papá waved. Mamá joined him, and he put his arm about her shoulder, pressing her to him. We all watched as the youngest member of our family left the plaza and San Antonio. On their return to the chili stand, my parents' conversation confirmed what I suspected.

"*Es solo un chámaco.* He is only a boy," I heard Mamá say.

"*Sabe más de los caballos que la mayoría de los hombres.* He knows more about horses than most men."

"*¿No podría haber esperado un par de años más?* Could he have waited a couple of years?"

"*Puede tener más éxito con Mr. Bishop que con nosotros.* He can do better with Mr. Bishop than he can with us. *No podemos esperar. Necesitamos sus ganancias ahora.* We cannot wait. We need his earnings now."

I wondered whether José would still be with us if I had been more successful making our chili stand profitable. We were doing better, but not yet good enough. And we still had Elena to pay. I had to find a way.

CHAPTER 15

"José has left us for a cattle drive," I explained to Peter the next night. Peter sipped hot chocolate, lowered the cup to its saucer, and looked intently at me with his striking eyes.

"He is very young. Your father agreed?"

I nodded. "Yes. It is what José wants to do. He is good with horses."

"Cattle drives will soon be a thing of the past. The railroads are more efficient and less expensive."

"Papá thinks that he can get a good job as a horse wrangler on a large ranch." I was reluctant to tell Peter the primary reason Papá agreed. Besides, I had learned it by eavesdropping on a conversation between Mamá and Papá.

Peter raised his eyebrows and took another sip of his drink. "I hope so." Then he changed the subject. "Lupe, there is going to be a demonstration of rifle marksmanship at San Pedro Springs Park on Sunday. Would you do me the honor of accompanying me? We can take the trolley as we did last time. Your father has given his permission if you wish to join me."

I felt my heartbeat quicken and tried to steady myself. "Gracias, Peter, I would like that very much."

"I will come for you on Sunday afternoon. Would you be able to leave a little earlier this time, at half past two? The shooting demonstration at the race track will begin at three."

"Sí. I can manage that."

"Josefa, also?"

"I will ask her."

"Then unless you tell me differently, I shall see you both on Sunday." He paid for his chocolate and, again, left me a penny tip.

I regretted that we could not yet afford to give him a free drink.

It was still early, still daylight on this Friday afternoon. Hopefully business would pick up after dark. As I continued setting up, I took stock of what I was doing to increase business: *The stories are beginning to attract new customers. Some said they came because they heard about the chili queen in the red and blue rebozo who tells interesting stories. With Josefa running off most nights and José gone, I need Elena's help more than ever. But how can we pay her? We cannot increase the price of our enchiladas, chili, tortillas, frijoles, coffee, chocolate, and smokes and stay competitive with other stands. Each serving is only a few cents. We have to sell more to increase income. Rebozos might help. It is almost time for señor Lopez to return from Mexico. I need money.*

"*¿Qué te tiene tan pensativa?* What has you so deep in thought?"

Antonio's question snapped me out of my musings.

"*Eres exactamente la persona que deseo ver.* You are just the man I wish to see." The time had come.

"Oh?" He smiled broadly. "*¿Qué pasa?*"

I blurted out, "I need a loan."

Antonio's eyes widened. "A loan? For what?"

"I have asked señor Lopez to bring me five beautiful rebozos from San Luis Potosí. You know, hand-loomed rebozos, distinctive in pattern and of good quality. I can sell them."

"What makes you think so?"

"I have one customer already. A sheep rancher who likes my rebozo and ordered one for his wife."

"He may be unique, Lupe. When was the last time you saw an American woman wearing a rebozo?"

"I am American and I wear one."

"Lupe, you are seen as Mexican."

"I was born on the King Ranch—in Texas."

"That does not matter as much as how you look, talk, and act. Look around you. Who wears the rebozo?"

I hated to admit that Antonio was making a point I had not thought about. "Anyway, most Mexican women we know cannot afford the type of rebozo you describe."

"My family has this one."

"*¡Uno!* An heirloom. Be realistic, Lupe."

"There are shawls for sale in the stores and catalogues. You see women in town wearing them. You can do many more things with a rebozo than with a shawl. Nice long rebozos can be used to carry things like groceries and babies. They cover the head, arms, and shoulders, keeping the wearer protected from the wind and drizzle. They can also add color to dark clothes. If señor Lopez brings me beautiful and unusual rebozos, maybe I can start a new trend. Women might exchange their shawls for rebozos."

"*Si y tal vez.* If and maybe."

"I think that it could happen."

I left to get him a plate of enchiladas and a cup of coffee. When I returned and set his meal in front of him, Antonio looked up at me and asked, "How much do you need?"

"At least fifteen dollars. Maybe as much as twenty-six and fifty if señor Lopez delivers the best."

"That is a lot of money, Lupe. Where would I get that much?"

"You have a regular job. I thought you made a good salary."

"I am still an apprentice. Right now, I make only enough to help my parents with living expenses. Not much is left to spend."

"Or gamble."

Antonio's eyes widened.

"You know that your reputation goes before you, Antonio. You are a shrewd and smart gambler."

"Maybe at the cockfights I could turn a few dollars."

"No."

"Why not?"

"We used to have a rooster and hens when we lived at Santa Gertrudis. El Gallo would rouse us at dawn every day. Papá said he was better than a church bell. It was my job to feed them. When I carried a tin of grain into the yard for them, el Gallo always came to me. He was a good-looking rooster with beautiful plumage."

"My cocks are different. They are bred to fight."

"You train them to fight and strap sharp spikes to their spurs."

"It is sport."

"Too cruel for me."

"I do well at the cockfights."

"I do not want blood money. You do well at cards. Maybe a poker game at the Washington Theater?"

Antonio shook his head. "Not there. Or anywhere else for a while."

"¿Por qué?"

Antonio averted his eyes.

"You were caught cheating?"

He did not answer.

"Tell me, Antonio. Were you?"

He refused to say, but I knew I had guessed right. He asked, "How much do you have?"

"Right now, I have one and sixty-five. In a few days, I can raise that to two dollars."

"Not very much, but a start. Let me think about this, Lupita."

"Señorita, will you tell your story about Quanah Parker this evening?"

As I turned toward the voice, the plaza was changing from market to fiesta. The softness of twilight erased the unsightly places. Lantern lights, dotting the chili stands, twinkled like stars strewn by an unseen wizard. The transformation was breathtaking.

"I came back just to hear that story," the cowboy said.

"And not to enjoy the best chile sauce on the plaza?"

"That too, of course."

"Some enchiladas?"

"I had those last night."

"Some chili then? With frijoles and tortillas?"

He nodded.

I looked around for Josefa. She motioned that she would serve him. Just as Elena arrived, I called to the passersby, "Would you like to hear a true story about Quanah Parker?"

A couple of army officers from the post seated themselves on a bench. "What about Quanah Parker?" one asked.

"Would you like something to eat first? Our enchiladas are the tastiest on the plaza. Our chile sauce is like no other. Smooth with just the right touch of heat. And only a nickel for three delicious tortillas—my mamá makes them fresh for each customer—smothered in our famous chile sauce and covered with crumbled fresh cheese and chopped onion. Mouthwatering! ¿Sí?"

"Sí, señorita, por favor."

Elena took their orders, helped Mamá prepare the soldiers' plates, and served, offering them hot coffee. They accepted. We now had five customers, enough to begin. I hoped that more would arrive as the evening matured.

I wrapped the rebozo about my shoulders and arms, fluttered its fringes, and as soon as I had everyone's attention, I began:

"Miguel and the cowhands had been driving the cattle up the Red River for several days. The grass was in good supply. So was the water. They got to the Wichita Mountains, and there they met Quanah Parker and his party of six braves. Over six feet tall, Quanah towered over his men and most of the cowboys. Even more so on his tall horse. Miguel felt small in his imposing presence. But it was more than sheer physical size. He carried himself with an air of dignity, Miguel recalled, holding himself erect whether standing or mounted. Quanah was dressed cowboy style in a well-shaped hat, shirt and pants. Miguel said that you could see his muscles ripple beneath his shirt. His hair, as black as ancho chiles, was parted in the middle. It hung half way down his chest in rolls wrapped in red cloth. His skin was copper colored. When he spoke, perfect teeth shone bright white against his dark complexion. But his most arresting feature, Miguel recalled, was his piercing gray-blue eyes. A six-shooter was holstered at his side. In contrast, his men were in breechcloths, armed with Winchesters. They looked fierce. If you wanted a fight, they would give you one to remember.

"Quanah greeted the men and asked to speak to the trail boss. He had come to collect payment for grazing rights on his territory. The toll was a yearling. The trail boss told Miguel to take Quanah to the horse herd to pick one out. Quanah made his selection and motioned his braves to drive the yearling to their camp. But Quanah stayed behind with a companion. They watched as the cowhands began driving cattle and horses across the swollen river. They watched as the men cut timber and tied logs together with rope for a makeshift raft to ferry the wagon across."

"They'd have to ferry it with ropes stretched across the river," a man said.

"You have done that?" I asked.

He nodded. "Sometimes horses refuse to swim. You have to raft them across, too."

"But this crew had a hard time. One by one, the men tried to swim the rope across the river. One by one, they would get halfway across, then have to turn the rope loose or risk drowning, and swim back. A cowhand got close enough to the opposite bank but lost the end of the rope and landed without it."

"Did any man succeed?" one of the soldiers asked.

"It took two."

"How?" his companion said.

"Miguel told me, 'I was the sixth man to try. I took the rope between my teeth, passing it over my shoulder. As I swam out, the boys on the bank slowly released the rope. The river was fighting me, and I went under once, twice, three times. Each time, I bounced to the surface, the rope held fast in my clenched teeth. I was halfway to the opposite bank when once again the current pulled me under. My arms ached. My fingers were numb. I thought I was a dead man.'"

I paused to make the moment more dramatic. I waited. My tale had attracted others who stopped to listen.

"'The river had knocked the fight out of me,' Miguel said, 'and I was about to give in to its power when I felt a strong force push me upward and propel me forward. I felt for the rope. It was still in my mouth. I was like a racehorse that was on the bit. I guess I was so determined, I just held on. The unknown force gripped me under my arms, and dragged me on my back through the water. I had no strength left to do anything but allow it to take me wherever it would. And then I felt myself being pulled out of the water face down, onto the dry bank. I opened my mouth to gasp for air and released the rope. I heard a cheer. My lungs ached. It felt like a tree had fallen on my chest. When I could breathe again, I rolled on my back and looked up into gray-blue eyes.'"

"Quanah Parker?" one of the soldiers guessed.

I nodded and smiled. "Miguel says that he will be forever grateful to that man for saving his life."

"And getting the ferry across," the cowboy added.

I nodded. "Still a bit unsteady, Miguel propped himself up, pushed his sopping wet hair back from his face, and felt for the small silver cross that hung around his neck on a leather thong. It was still there. He lifted it over his head and offered it to Quanah Parker. 'My mother gave this to me,' he said.

"Quanah's eyes flickered."

"His mother, Cynthia Ann Parker, had been taken back to her kin with his baby sister after Quanah's Comanche father and brother were killed," one of the soldiers said.

"She wasn't content apart from the Comanches," the other added.

"Miguel told Quanah, 'I would like you to have it to remember me by.'

"Quanah said nothing but he hung the cross around his neck. He returned to the riverbank where his man was waiting. Miguel never saw him again, but he remembered him for the rest of his life."

I held out my arms, fringes aflutter, and bowed to signal the end of my story.

"I enjoyed that, señorita," the cowboy said.

"So did I," another added.

The soldiers offered me penny tips that I accepted with a smile and curtsy. "You are a good storyteller. We'll be back to hear more."

The stand emptied as the first wave of diners finished their meals and left in search of other amusements on the plaza. Elena was collecting used dishes and utensils and wiping down the oilcloth. In the distance, I could hear the Fashion Theater's brass band warming up. I looked around for Josefa and guessed that she had gone off again to find the actor. *I must talk to her soon about that.*

"Was your father really saved by Quanah Parker?" Antonio was resting his elbows on the table, deliberately making it difficult for Elena to wipe his area. He was toying with her cloth like a kitten chasing feathers.

"He did meet Quanah on the trail at the place where I said, the north fork of the Red River near the Wichita Mountains."

"But he didn't almost drown."

"Yes, he did. He carried that ferry rope across the river just as I described."

Antonio shot me a crooked smile.

I relented. "Yes, I embellished the event a bit. A story should get better with each telling, even if that means stretching the truth a little."

He waved his hand as if to clear the air. "*Tengo una idea.*"

"*¿Sobre qué?* About what?"

"*Hace tu dinero crecer.* Making your money grow."

CHAPTER 16

An advantage to working nights is that I rarely felt summer heat. The hottest days usually transformed into pleasant evenings. But on this mid-August Sunday afternoon, there was no relief. Even the cotton bodice I had was long sleeved and high necked, as fashion and modesty required. I spot bathed after midday dinner, then rubbed crushed rosemary leaves from our garden over the back of my neck and wrists. I suffered the heat waiting for Peter to arrive.

"Lupita. Here he comes," Josefa called. It was exactly two-thirty when he knocked on the door.

He brought a tin of tea leaves for Mamá and a cigar for Papá, greeted my siblings who had come for Sunday dinner and, I think, to see Peter again. He escorted Josefa and me to Acequia Street where we caught the trolley. This time, the mule stayed on track and we arrived at San Pedro Springs Park in plenty of time to watch the shooting match.

A large number of onlookers had assembled on the viewing stand at the racetrack. Peter found seats for us, and after we were settled, he pointed out the two men with Winchesters who were conversing near several crates. He identified one as Mr. Penrose, who had challenged the other, Dr. Carver, to the shooting match. The object was to see which could shoot the most out of a set of one hundred birds. I guessed that doves were in the crates.

"Some are making bets on the outcome," Peter said, nodding to a tight group of men in animated conversation.

"Who do you think will win?" a familiar voice asked. It was Tom O'Malley's.

Peter extended his hand to Tom, who had asked the people sitting next to Josefa to move down the bench a bit to give him a seat.

"Well, Dr. Carver has demonstrated his marksmanship on more than one occasion here, including shooting while on horseback. But Mr. Penrose is the challenger. My guess is that he thinks he can do better."

"Will you bet on him, then?" Tom asked.

Peter shook his head, "I'm not a betting man."

"Hold this place for me," Tom said to Josefa. "I'm going to make a wager." He snaked his way across the rows of spectators to where the bookmakers offered odds. There was a transfer of notes and then he was back, sitting close to Josefa, his hand resting on hers.

I did not like seeing birds set free only to be shot in midair and fall to the ground, but many of the spectators cheered with each kill. Several were keeping audible count. Mr. Belknap kept the official count and announced the score. Carver: eighty-one hits. Penrose: ninety.

Tom let out a whoop. "Thanks, Peter," he said. "Come on, Josefa. We can celebrate with my winnings."

Josefa turned to me and whispered, "I will meet you at the beer garden in about an hour."

Before I could respond, she and Tom were gone.

"Have you talked to her about this, Lupe?"

"When she first began to see him, but not recently."

"You need to do so again. Soon."

I nodded, disappointed with myself for not dealing with the problem.

"Now, would you like a beer?"

At the beer garden, Peter found a tree-shaded table where he seated me and left to get our drinks. A band was playing a waltz. Dancers filled the pavilion despite the heat. When Peter returned, he placed a frosty glass of sparkling amber liquid in front of me. The refreshing drink cooled me from the first sip.

"How is business?" he asked.

"Improved. My stories seem to be attracting a few more customers."

"You see, Lupe, I was right. You are the bard of Military Plaza. I could listen to you all night."

"But our profits are not greatly increased."

"How do you know?"

"Our benches are well filled every night, to be sure. Our customers do appear to enjoy my stories. But they do not buy more than a plate and a drink and maybe a smoke each night. They just stay."

"You may be right, Lupe, but your judgment is based on impression. The only way you can be certain about your income is to keep a ledger. You have to record your costs and compare that total with your sales."

Peter pulled a small sheet of paper and a stubby pencil from his breast pocket. "What ingredients do you use? We should list all the ingredients you purchase, how much of each you use and at what cost—enough for a week."

"If they all order the same thing?"

"No. To be accurate, we should take each dish separately. Chiles, for instance, how many chiles do you buy to make sauce?"

I looked at him sideways. "Are you trying to get our secret recipe?"

Peter took me seriously. He frowned and started to put the pencil and paper back into his jacket pocket.

"No, Peter, wait." I laughed and reached out to catch his arm. "I was teasing. Start again, por favor."

I thought he might be piqued. He said nothing, just took a sip of his beer, placed the paper on the table, and positioned the pencil in his hand. "Chiles?"

"Six anchos and four guajillos and four pasillas every day. Sometimes more, double or triple, depending on how much sauce we think we will need."

"We'll start with your basic recipe. We can multiply as you increase the yield. That would be thirty-six anchos, and twenty-four each of guajillos and pasillas for a six-day workweek. How much do you pay for them?"

"Mamá buys them from the chile vendors on the plaza."

"Ask her the cost."

I nodded. "Garlic."

"How much?

"Five cloves. About a third of a medium-size bulb each night. That would be two bulbs per week."

"What do you pay for them?"

I shrugged. " Mamá . . ."

"Mr. Kotula sells garlic in his store for two cents a bulb."

"I tapped my index finger on the tabletop, a signal for Peter to record that cost, four cents, on his list.

"What else?"

"Sometimes we add a little chile piquin, but we harvest those from wild bushes. We grow our own oregano. We use salt, of course, and lard. But only a little of each."

"You have to record everything to be accurate, Lupe. Mr. Kotula sells sugar at one and five for three pounds and lard at thirty-eight cents for two pounds. Pepper and salt are a dollar a sack."

"For the chile sauce, we use no more than three teaspoons of salt and even less sugar, and a few tablespoons of lard each night. We do go through several pounds of *masa de maíz* for . . . "

"The tasty tortillas your mother makes. Mr. Kotula sells a five-pound bag of wheat flour for one and eighty. I will check on the cost of masa de maiz. I know that you use onions and queso fresco. You buy those from the local vendors, too?"

I nodded.

"I'll add coffee to the list. You buy that from me at thirty-five cents a pound. I would estimate that you use an ounce for every three to four cups."

"That would amount to six cents for nine or ten."

"Right. Costing you about one and a half cents for two servings." Peter wrote on the paper. He pushed it toward me. "The coffee is a good example. If our estimates are correct, you make a little over a penny for each cup you sell. That is what we need to find out about your other sales. Ask your mother what she pays for all the ingredients on the list and how much of each you use at your chili stand each week. With that we can calculate your costs. The difference between that figure and your selling price will show your profit. Keep track of the number of diners and what they order each week. That information will help you to decide how to make your business profitable." He drained his mug.

I folded Peter's list carefully and tucked it under the cuff on my left sleeve.

"That's enough of business," he said. "Would you like to dance?"

I nodded and Peter escorted me to the dance floor. The orchestra was playing a waltz and I leaned into his right hand at the small of my back. We danced until the music stopped, but Peter did not release his hold. Another waltz began. I again felt the slight pressure of his hand on my back, guiding me across the dance floor. I began to hum the familiar tune and relaxed in Peter's arms, enjoying the pleasure of being close to him.

"A good band, don't you think?" The cheerful voice was on my right. "Come on," it said. "I'll buy us all a beer with my winnings."

"Lupe, the four of us can visit," I heard Josefa say.

Peter whispered, "Let him. We can stay for a little while longer and then it will be time to head home."

I was disappointed. I had hoped to have Peter all to myself for the rest of the afternoon. We found another table to seat four and settled there while Tom and Peter brought the drinks.

Tom took a seat on Josefa's right and dropped his left hand below the table. I saw Josefa do the same with her right and guessed they were holding hands.

"I will be leaving San Antonio in a few days," Tom told us. I glanced at Josefa. She did not seem startled by the news.

"Where are you headed?" Peter asked.

"Saint Louis. I will perform at a vaudeville theater there for a few weeks, then move on to Chicago, and then to New York City."

"You will be gone for a long while, then?" I asked.

Tom nodded. "But I'll be back. You can be sure of that." He smiled at Josefa.

"Why do you like the theater?" Peter asked.

"I know no other life. My parents were show people. We moved from town to town, city to city with a traveling road show. I was on stage at four. We danced and sang. My father told jokes. My mother had a singing voice that I never tired of hearing. Men were always waiting to see her after the show."

"Where is your family now?" I asked.

He paused and his smile drained away. "My mother ran off with a man she met who said he was going to make her a star. After that, my father sank into melancholia. He found solace in drink. I was sixteen when he died. An only child with no kin, I was on my own. I needed work. All I knew how to do was sing and dance. I performed on street corners for tips, begged saloon owners to give me work, and ended up joining a traveling vaudeville group. The audiences liked me and in time, my name was known on the vaudeville circuit. I got to play at theaters all over the country, some in big cities. I've been doing that ever since."

"It must be distressing to have no roots," Peter said.

"You get used to it. After a while, you look forward to the next stop. Every place is different. Besides, it pays my bills." Tom laughed. "To be honest, I like to be in the limelight. Singing and dancing are like breathing for me. And when the audience applauds, I feel important, appreciated . . . loved." He grew pensive for a moment. "I will miss your sister, though. But this is a good opportunity for me."

My throat tightened.

"I think it's time we headed back," Peter said.

Tom rode the trolley with us, whispering to Josefa the whole way. He helped her off at our stop, kissed her hand, and said goodbye. Josefa watched him walk away. Peter and I waited. When she approached us, moist eyes gave her away.

CHAPTER 17

By the time we returned home, most of our family had left. Mamá and Papá were visiting with Elena's parents. Peter thanked me for a fine time, bid us goodbye, and went next door to thank our parents before departing. The house was empty and I saw my chance.

"*¿Me quieres acompañar con una taza de café?* Will you join me in a cup of coffee?" I asked Josefa.

"*Sí. Me gustaría.* Yes, that would be nice." She sat wearily on a bench in the yard and propped her elbows on the table, supporting her head with her hands as she watched me.

The embers were still hot. It took no time to rekindle the cook fire. I put several teaspoons of ground coffee and a stick of cinnamon into the coffeepot and poured in water from the *aquador,* the barrel filled weekly with drinking water. When the water came to a strong simmer, just short of boiling, I removed the pot from the heat. I placed a few crushed eggshells Mamá saved into a small amount of cool water. This I added to the pot to help settle the grounds. I let the brew sit for a few minutes before pouring us each a cup. I sat across the table from Josefa and broached the subject slowly.

"It was a pleasant afternoon. I hardly felt the heat at San Pedro Springs Park."

"Because you were with Peter," she said. "You enjoy being with him so much that you do not think about the weather."

I nodded. "Is it the same for you with Tom O'Malley?"

Josefa's face flushed and her eyes filled with tears. "I love him, Lupe."

"You know that is dangerous for you?"

She could not control the tears any longer. They streamed down her face. "I know. He lives a drifter's life. But he promised me he would come back."

"Do you think he means that, Josefa?"

She wiped her face and nose with a handkerchief. "Oh, yes. He has told me many times of his love for me."

"How good is his word?"

"I believe him."

"What do you hope for?"

"I want to marry him."

"Have you shared your feelings with Mamá and Papá?"

She shook her head. "He has not yet spoken of marriage. But he will. I know he will."

"What makes you think so?"

Josefa's eyes met mine. She paused and I tried to read her expression. Her whisper was so soft I could not hear what she was saying and asked her to repeat. With a catch in her throat she told me, "We have been intimate."

I rushed around to her side of the table to embrace her. She buried her face against me and wept. Her sobbing was quiet and controlled, but I felt her trembling.

I held my sister for a long time until we heard our parents enter the house. I took her inside, helped her undress, and put her to bed. When I went back into the yard, Mamá and Papá were drinking the coffee left in the pot.

"*¿Te divertiste?* Did you have a good time?" Papá asked.

I nodded, filled my cup and joined them. "*Tuvimos un día muy activo.* We had an active day. Josefa is tired out and has gone to bed. San Pedro Springs Park is a lovely place. And Peter is a thoughtful companion."

"He seems very nice," Mamá said.

Papá added, "*Pero es diferente a nosotros.* But he is different from us."

"There is much that we have in common," I added quickly.

"He speaks Spanish well," Mamá said. "And he has plans for a good future."

"In what way are you thinking about him?" Papá asked.

"I am not sure." I was being honest. "I enjoy his company. We need to get to know one another better."

"That is wise, Lupita," Papá said. "Quick judgments can ruin a life."

I knew he would give the same advice to Josefa and quickly changed the subject. "Elena has been a big help at the stand. I hope she will continue."

"We were discussing that with señora and señor Hernández. They are agreeable but would like her to earn more than tips for her efforts," Papá said.

"*De acuerdo*. I agree. What can we afford to offer?"

Papá shook his head. "Not as much as her parents would like. You are doing a good job bringing more diners to the table, Lupe, but our income is still small. Mamá tells me that they come to hear your stories. They order one dish. Maybe they add a drink and a smoke. We need them to order more or leave so that others can take their seats and buy meals."

"*Lo sé*. I know, Papá. I am working on that. I really need Elena to help serve so that I can entertain more. Peter suggested that I keep a ledger to have a precise list of expenses and income. It can help us see if we are making a profit." I pulled out the accounting list Peter had begun. Papá looked at it.

"Buena idea," he said. "He is a bright young man. Mamá can help you fill in our costs. We can keep track of how much we sell in the coming weeks. Then we can suggest a salary for Elena."

Over the next days, I saw Mamá talking with Josefa on several occasions, but Josefa told me they had not discussed her relationship with the actor. She swore me to secrecy, and I agreed with the stipulation that she would always confide in me first. I was worried about Josefa, even though she seemed her normal self on many outings with Peter, who took us on long walks, picnics, and to band concerts. I thought she might be putting on a brave face.

The Sunday afternoons I spent with Peter reduced the time I had to listen to Papá's stories, so my repertoire remained limited to those I had told before. I embellished them with each telling, and my audiences remained interested. Customers even requested stories they had heard before. Some ordered one meal and nothing more, though they stayed to hear my story and sing along with us. Others came for the stories and bought nothing. I could not demand that they buy something or chase them away if they did not. I had a stand full of people, but without a substantial increase in sales. And now with Josefa back, I no longer really needed Elena's help. Yet my parents had agreed to pay her a salary before long, and I did not want them to lose face. Besides, Elena was a much better server than Josefa had ever been. I did not expect Tom O'Malley to return. But I knew that if he did, I could not rely on Josefa's help. I had taken on the task of improving the chili stand's profits. It was turning out to be more complicated than I had imagined. All I could think to do now was to find another way. *¿Los rebozos?*

Standing on San Fernando's front steps after Sunday Mass, I scanned Main Plaza. An animated cluster of people gathered around Antonio Ortiz. He held a lead line attached to a bridle on the imposing head of a very tall horse. I skipped down the church steps and headed toward that gathering. Antonio waved and motioned me forward.

I was accustomed to old and worn-out horses that spent their lives hauling heavily loaded wagons. Antonio's filly was tall—about seventeen hands—a blood bay with black points and a feather-like white star on her forehead. Her mane shone in the midday sunshine that played over her muscled shoulder and broad rump. Her tail, like her mane, was of mixed black, brown, and red hues. It cascaded from dock to fetlock. Her body was firm and tucked up. She had no hay belly like the horses I knew. Her head was fine, her chocolate-colored eyes alert and commanding. They had the look of an eagle's.

The filly let me touch her velvety black muzzle.

"*¿Dónde la consiguió?* Where did you get her?" I asked.

"*Tuve suerte.* I was lucky. A cattle rancher from south of town asked me if I would trim and shoe his team of wagon horses in return for this thoroughbred filly. He won her in a poker game. She's three years old with good bloodlines and broke to bridle, saddle, and rider, smart and fast."

"*Este es una yegua fina.* This is a fine filly," Papá said. "*Pero, ella es demasiado buena para tirar de un carreta.* But she is too good to pull a cart. So what will you do with her? How will she earn her keep?"

"*Es un caballo de carreras.* She is a racehorse," Antonio said. "I will race her. With this filly, I can become rich."

"You could lose more than you gain."

"That depends on the races."

"You want a race?" A voice from the outside the growing crowd called out.

Antonio strained his neck to see the speaker.

"Here," the man said and waved. "I can arrange a match race for you."

"Not yet," Antonio answered. "I have to make preparations."

"Well, let me know when you're ready. You can find me at the poker tables in the Washington."

"She seems very calm to be a racehorse," one of the spectators said.

Antonio nodded. "Wait until she gets some grain and we begin exercising. You will see her energy peak."

"And when will you have time to do this work?" I asked.

"Early in the morning, before Mr. Illg expects me at the smithy."

Some of the young men in the group laughed.

"You think I cannot do it?"

"We know you will try," one of them answered. "But it is a lot, even for you."

"Just wait and see." Antonio shot me a knowing look, then turned to my parents. "*¿Te gustaría verla correr?* Would you like to see her gallop?"

"*Después de la comida.* After dinner," Papá said. "Join us. Then we will all go to watch your filly."

"Gracias, señor Pérez. I would like that. I will put her up in one of Mr. Illg's stalls, then join you. There's a nice stretch of road on the city's outskirts where she can run."

"Bueno. That will be good," Papá said. "¡Vamos!" he said to us. "We will have some good entertainment this afternoon."

Mamá leaned toward me and whispered, "You should ask your papá about his days racing with Comanches on the trail."

After dinner was eaten and the dishes washed and stacked, Mamá, Papá, Josefa, Elena, señor and señora Hernández and I walked with Antonio to Mr. Illg's stables. Antonio's younger brother, Juan, was waiting for us with the filly, groomed to a high gloss and tacked up in the bridle, bit, and racing saddle that had come with her. We fell in behind as Antonio and Juan led her along San Pedro Creek to the dirt road north of town.

"Juan will take her for a gallop to the bridge across the San Antonio River where Rock Quarry Road becomes Josephine Street," he told us. "Find a place along that route."

We walked along Rock Quarry Road to the bridge. Each of us picked a place to watch. Papá waved to Antonio. I saw Juan, now mounted, walk the filly forward, hasten her into trot, then canter, and finally, full gallop. She was running fast now, neck stretched forward, ears perked, with her tongue lolling out the side of her mouth. She thundered by us, a dark streak. I felt the ground rumble beneath my feet. Her breathing was strong and cadenced. She was moving like a well-tuned engine.

Papá whistled his appreciation. Señor Hernández whooped. Mamá clapped. Señora Hernández cheered. Beside me, Elena was bouncing in place.

Antonio ran toward us from the starting point, looking down the road. I followed his line of sight. The filly was cantering back. Juan slowed her to a walk as she passed.

"*Miren esta cabriole*. Look at that prance," Papá said. "She is on her toes. She knows what she can do." He took Antonio's hands in his own. "¡Felicitaciones! You must give her a good name."

"*Ya lo he hecho. Se llama la Reina.* I have. She is called the Queen."

Papá grinned. "*¿Cuándo correrá?* When will she race?"

CHAPTER 18

In mid-September, when temperatures were beginning to ease, the gambler who had been on Main Plaza the Sunday Antonio first showed off his filly arranged the match race. He offered to double Antonio's money if la Reina could beat a three-year-old colt named el Soldado.

"Are you sure this is a fair match?" I asked Antonio when he told me of the plan.

"Sí. She has trained well and is at peak level. Trust me. I know my filly. She can make your money grow."

Since first talking with Antonio about the rebozos, I had collected a total of three and fifty in tips. Elena added two dollars more. If we could double that, I would have half of what I needed to pay señor Lopez. He was due back in San Antonio in October, only about four weeks hence.

On race day, a large crowd assembled at the San Pedro Springs Park racetrack to watch and wager. Word of a race had traveled throughout the park. People streamed onto the grounds from the beer garden and the picnic tables. Mamá and Papá were among them. So were my sisters and brothers and their families, all the neighbors up and down Laredo Street, and the merchants and vendors from Military Plaza. Mr. Wulff was there. So were Peter and Mr. Kotula. Peter told me that his employer had helped to reserve the racetrack for the race. Antonio had talked to Peter who had asked Mr. Kotula. And so it was done.

Juan steadied la Reina. Gilberto Gonzalez was mounted on the chestnut colt. Both horses were on the muscle, ready to run after their warmups.

Their riders walked them to and from the starting line until John Illg, the designated starter, signaled them to approach.

A single shot. Sudden quiet. Then the roar began, gathering volume down the line of spectators in the stands.

I strained to see. The two forms, riders and horses, were running close together at the first turn. As they moved onto the far side of the track, the chestnut surged forward. The bay filly was just a head behind.

The horses were coming closer now. People were yelling. My heart was throbbing. At the start of the near turn, la Reina was still trailing el Soldado. Juan leaned over her neck, whipping the reins. The filly surged forward to challenge el Soldado's lead. As they cleared the turn for the stretch, the two were neck and neck. "¡Vamos, la Reina!" I yelled.

Gilberto brought his quirt down hard on the colt's rump, then his shoulder. Even over the crowd's din, I heard the thunder of hooves striking the ground near where I stood. I held my breath. They were now within a few feet of the finish line. In those last split seconds, Juan waved his quirt rapidly back and forth past la Reina's her right eye to urge her on, then swung it back to strike her rump, and the filly accelerated, passing el Soldado by a nose over the finish line. I screamed my delight. Elena threw her arms around me and we bounced together in place.

The winner was congratulated and the loser made excuses. Bettors collected their winnings or lamented their bad luck. Horsemen debated the merits of the racers and how they had been ridden. The horses were cooled and rubbed down. The riders described their trips to the owners. The owners vowed to run a rematch. After all that, Antonio showed me the winnings. Elena and I now had eleven dollars. It was double what we started with, although still not as much as I expected señor Lopez to charge for the rebozos—if he came back with rebozos.

Antonio put the eleven dollars, a fistful of bills and coins, into my hand. "I know that you need more than this. La Reina went into this race an unknown. Her odds will be shorter next time. I will not be able to make your money grow so fast. So I have decided to lend you my winnings." He counted out eleven dollars and added them to the eleven I already held. "Now you should have enough to buy those rebozos."

"Thank you, Antonio. Your kindness touches my heart."

He looked at me intently. "I hope so," he said. His voice was tender. He was silent, his eyes searching my face. When he spoke again, his tone had changed. "Remember, Lupe, this is not a gift. I am investing in your business and I expect repayment with interest." But he winked and shot me a crooked smile. I was not sure what to make of that.

"Of course, Antonio. I shall repay you and Elena for helping me."

"*¡Buena suerte!* Good luck." He cupped my hands over the money.

Elena tugged on my sleeve. "Mine is a gift," she said. "I do not expect repayment."

"That is very generous of you," Peter said. "But it should not be necessary. If Lupe is correct, a good profit can be made off the rebozos, enough to pay her debts and to build the business.

"*¡Basta!* Enough!" Antonio said. "It is time to celebrate my filly's victory. I have arranged with Mr. Kerble to stable the racehorses in his livery. Listen. A band is playing at the pavilion. We can celebrate at the beer garden, and maybe señoras Pérez and Hernández will honor me with a dance." Antonio offered one arm to Mamá and the other to señora Hernández. The rest of us fell in behind in a boisterous procession away from the racetrack, marching to the beat of the band.

Señor Lopez was back in town. One of his customers who sold Mexican chiles on the plaza delivered his message. The next morning, spurred on by the early chill of a typical October cooldown, I dressed hurriedly. From the bottom of the clothes trunk, I retrieved the small string-tied burlap pouch that had once held tobacco. It was tucked inside one of my stockings. I emptied the pouch onto my lap and counted the collection of bills and coins. I had exactly twenty-two dollars. I put the money back into the pouch, tied it to one end of my rebozo, and headed for South Laredo and Arsenal.

"¡Hola! señor Lopez."

"¡Hola! Lupe. You came quickly."

"*He estado esperando los rebozos.* I have been waiting for the rebozos."

"*He traído unos muy bonitos.* I have brought some beautiful ones. You have the money?"

I nodded.

"*¡Mira!* Look."

He pulled a package from inside his wagon. "Go ahead. Open it."

My fingers fumbled over the knot in the string. Once loosened, the paper wrapping fell away revealing a pile of colorful rebozos. One by one, señor Lopez draped each over his arm. "The colors are bright. The weaves are fine. And look at the fringes, long and intricate."

I fingered one with stripes of violet and lime green set off by an indigo background. It was handsome, but the thread was coarse. "This cotton is not as fine as I had hoped for."

"But the dyes are bright. And it is not expensive. I can let you have it for three dollars."

"What about this one?" I picked up a silky white rebozo with an intriguing pink zigzag pattern and fringes a foot long.

"You have good taste. That is one of my finest."

"How much?"

"Six and fifty."

Just those two would take almost half my money. "That is expensive," I said.

"You need the right customer for this rebozo, someone who appreciates its value. You could charge double its cost."

"I do not know. Let me see the others."

Señor Lopez showed me another cotton rebozo of bright orange and deep blue. Its fringes were not long, but they were knotted in an unusual pattern. He set the price at three and fifty. Then there was one of black wool, its triangular design woven with red, gold, and aqua threads. He would sell me the black wool for four dollars and thirty. The last was a brilliant red and green silk. Its bright colors were separated by white with a slender gold accent thread running down its center. Tassels decorated each end. Señor Lopez asked six dollars. I struggled to hold the numbers in my head to find their total, twenty-three and thirty.

"I do not have enough for all of them," I told him.

"I told you they would not be cheap."

"I can buy four of them."

"You ordered five. What am I going to do with one rebozo?"

"I can give you twenty dollars for all five."

"They are worth twenty-three."

"Twenty-one."

"Twenty-two and fifty."

"Twenty-one and fifty."

"Twenty-two."

"Done."

I emptied the tobacco pouch and counted out the money into señor Lopez's hand. He double counted, then nodded, rewrapped the rebozos and handed me the package.

"You know how to bargain, Lupe. I hope you get a good return on these. *¡Buena suerte!*"

I was now faced with a dilemma. Should I offer the rebozos for sale before Mr. Johnson returned? Or should I keep them hidden so he could have first choice? That seemed the fair thing to do as he had given me the idea, but it was not good business. I had no guarantee that he would return soon or that he would buy one. Fortunately, I did not have to choose. Mr. Johnson arrived at my stand that week. The rebozos were still in their paper wrapper when he ordered a plate of enchiladas and coffee.

"Señorita Pérez, have you been able to find a rebozo for me? I'd like to make a present of one to my wife. This is my last visit to San Antonio before our anniversary."

"You are in luck, señor. The other day, I picked them up from the freighter. He had just returned from Mexico."

"One of the last, I guess. The mule-team freighter cannot compete with the railroad."

I nodded as I poured his coffee.

"May I see the rebozo?"

"I have five very nice ones for you to choose from."

I unfolded each rebozo and modeled it for him. He chose the one I thought he might like best, the white silk rebozo with the pink pattern and extra long fringes. He asked the cost. I offered it at ten dollars, expecting him to bargain. He did not. I had just earned three and fifty, better than half of the purchase cost.

Mr. Johnson folded the rebozo and tucked it under his arm. "My wife will be pleased. Gracias, señorita Pérez." He tipped his hat and left.

A man and woman took seats on the bench near where Mr. Johnson had sat. "What was it that rancher just bought from you?" the man asked.

I unfolded the orange and blue one. "It was a rebozo—a present for his wife—like this one. It will make a nice Christmas gift. I can let you have it for five and fifty."

The man shook his head. "Sorry, señorita. That is a bit dear for us. But I can afford a plate of the enchiladas like he had—one for my wife and one for me, por favor."

As more people arrived, I showed the rebozos. Elena and I modeled them. But no one was interested.

One man commented, rudely I thought, "I don't know any woman who would wear that."

"Many women wear shawls," I said. "The rebozo's length and width makes it more versatile than a shawl. It can warm a lady and be decorative, too."

"To be honest, señorita, I have only small coins in my pocket. You need to sell to richer men than me."

Another said, "We came for a good meal and a story. When will you tell your story tonight?"

"Yes, a story," another shouted.

Soon everyone at the stand was chanting, "A story. A story. A story."

From my collection of Papá's experiences on the range, I remembered the perfect one. Throwing the red and green silk rebozo over my shoulders, I fluttered the tassels, held out my arms and waited for attention. Then, I began:

"It happened on the south side of Red Fork, Oklahoma. The cattle had not been watered for two days. When the thirsty animals finally smelled water, they were anxious to get to it. But the high bluffs on the south side were impassable. They would have to travel over Indian land to reach the river.

"The drive came upon a city of tepees made of dressed and smoked buffalo hides. They blocked passage to the river. It was a Tonkawa village. The trail boss told the cook to separate some flour, coffee, and bacon, enough for three meals, and store it in the caboose."

I caught a quizzical look on a couple of faces. "You know," I explained, "the cowhide stretched under the wagon where they usually carried the Dutch oven, camp kettle, and the firewood collected on the trail. He told Miguel to wear his Mexican sash and ride alongside him."

I lowered the rebozo from around my shoulders, gathered its full width and wrapped it around my waist, knotting it on one side with the tassels skirting the ground. I continued:

"A party of armed, painted, and mounted braves emerged from the village, led by their chief in full war paint. A shield was fastened to the back of his hair, ornamented with many types of feathers. Two of his wives rode behind him holding the tails of his feathered headdress off the ground. Miguel estimated that they were about ten feet in length.

"The chief asked for flour, bacon, sugar, and coffee. The boss told the cook to set the requested supplies on the ground by the chuck wagon. Two of the chief's braves loaded the provisions on a pony and drove it back to their village.

"The wind shifted and the cattle became restless. Concerned that they might stampede, the trail boss decided to cross the river. He signaled his men to move the herd. But the braves who had stayed behind started roughhousing, whipping the cowboys' mounts, and the horses shied. They would not move. The drive was stalled.

"The chief said that his braves could help but he would need a larger toll. 'How much more?'

"'Everything you have.'

"Hoping they would not think to check the caboose, the trail boss agreed. The chief ordered a couple of braves to empty the chuck wagon. They hurled on the ground every sack, box, and tin of provisions they could find while others loaded them onto a pack animal—everything except the provisions hidden in the caboose.

"The chief asked for three large steers. They were given to him. Still not satisfied, he pointed to Miguel. 'You cannot have my man,' the trail boss said. The chief laughed when he understood the objection, making it known that it was not Miguel he wanted, but his sash.

"'Give it to him,' the trail boss said, 'and make a show of it.' Miguel removed the rebozo, unfurling it to full length. He recalled that the sunlight at that moment made its bright colors vivid. A breeze caught the rebozo's end, fluttering the tassels."

I stopped to show off my rebozo. I hoped that someone might want to buy it after the story.

"Miguel presented the rebozo to the chief. He wrapped it around his waist, adjusted the ends to cascade over the side of his horse, its tassels dangling at his foot. Satisfied with the toll, he let the drive cross, sending his braves to help hasten the rear cattle into the river. When all were safely on the far bank, the boss rode up to Miguel. 'That Mexican sash saved the herd—and the last of our provisions,' he told him. '¡Muchas gracias!'

"'Of course,' Miguel said. 'Magic threads were woven into it.'"

I removed the rebozo from around my waist and draped it over my shoulders, fluttering the tassels. "You can have the magic in this one for only eight dollars."

But no one was interested.

CHAPTER 19

"*Lupe, tengo que hablar contigo.* Lupe, I must talk with you," Josefa said. "Privately." There was urgency in her voice. Worry in her eyes.

"*Tan pronto que llegamos a casa.* As soon as we get home," I told her. "The coming rain will close us down soon. We will have plenty of time to talk at home."

Threatening skies had emptied the plaza early this night. We had no business. We packed in haste as dark billowing clouds formed. We arrived home just ahead of the rain. Papá hurriedly unhitched, fed, and watered Caballo. Elena and I unpacked the wagon. Mamá and Josefa carried supplies into the house.

"Where do you want to talk?" There were no really private places in our house.

"If we go to bed early, we can talk quietly there."

Mamá offered us coffee but we declined, saying we were tired. We stripped down to our chemises and crawled under the covers. The rain was beating on the roof. I pulled the blanket up over us both, then turned on my side to face Josefa.

"I am in trouble," she said. Her whisper quavered.

"Does this have something to do with Tom O'Malley?"

"Yes. I do not know what to do."

"About what?"

Josefa did not respond right away. I waited. When she began again, she spoke so softly I could not make out her words, even though our faces were only inches apart.

"I cannot hear you, Josefa."

In a slightly louder whisper she said, "I think I am going to have a baby."

A shudder ran through me. "Are you sure?"

"I have missed my woman's time for two months now."

That explained why I had not seen Josefa washing out her rags for some time. "The father is the actor?"

"He is the only man I have slept with."

"Did he say when he might return?"

"No, but he told me he would."

"When, Josefa?"

"I do not know. After many months, perhaps a year."

"The baby will be born by then. Does he know?"

"No. What am I going to do?"

"You must tell Mamá."

"She will be disappointed in me."

"Yes, but she will want to protect you."

"Mamá will say that I have brought disgrace to the family."

"Mamá will expect you to speak to your confessor at San Fernando and seek divine forgiveness. You must pray to Our Lady of Guadalupe. Place an offering at her altar."

"I cannot have a baby here. Everyone knows that I am unmarried. What will happen to me, Lupe?"

"Mamá will talk to Papá and they will know what to do. For now, try to get some sleep. Tomorrow, we will make a plan." I put my arms around my sister and drew her close to me. But we did not sleep long or well. Josefa wept, ashamed and frustrated. I wondered what would happen to her and her baby and our family.

The next day, I again urged Josefa to speak with Mamá soon. When we joined her in the yard to help make the chile sauce, I saw an opportunity. "*Puedo hacerlo, Mamá*. I can do that, Mamá. Josefa needs to talk to you—in private."

Mamá furrowed her brow. "*En privado?*"

"Si, Mamá," Josefa said. "*De algo muy importante*. About something very important."

Mamá washed and wiped her hands on a towel and motioned Josefa inside. I heard Josefa's soft whisper but could not hear her words, although I knew what she must have been saying. There was a long silence before Mamá responded, also in low tones. A pause and then muffled sobs. When both women returned to the yard, Mamá's face was drawn taut. Josefa's eyes were red and puffy.

"Josefa tells me that you know, Lupe."

I nodded.

"As soon as your father returns, we must tell him. He will help us decide what to do."

That evening, I saw the tightness around Papá's eyes and his mouth when he hitched Caballo to the wagon. He now knew, too. I did not ask. Josefa would tell me later.

Shadows danced across the plaza as the sun set on another spring-like November day. Elena set the table and lit the lamps. Their flames flickered dimly, brightening as the plaza darkened. "Look at the lamp in the sky," she said. "It is competing with our lanterns."

I looked skyward. A full moon brightened the night sky, helped by uncountable points of twinkling light.

"What a beautiful evening," she said. "I am so glad to be here."

"We have to try to sell these rebozos, Elena."

"Then give me one to wear."

"Which one?"

"The one you wore when you told the story of the rebozo that got the herd across the river."

I smiled and pulled it from the package to hand her.

Elena draped the rebozo around her shoulders and made the tassels dance like marionettes. She twirled in place. "This rebozo makes me feel pretty."

"You do not need a rebozo for that," Antonio said as he slid onto a bench at our table.

"Gracias, señor." Elena curtsied, flushed, and flipped one end of the rebozo over her shoulder. It seemed to embolden her. "Your usual?"

Antonio nodded and Elena called an order of enchiladas to Mamá while she poured his coffee, a steady twirl of steam rising from the surface of the dark liquid.

"It is little more than a month until Christmas," he said to me. "Are you having a *Tamalada?*"

"Of course." I hoped that this annual tradition would not be interrupted by Josefa's situation. *Las Posadas* was celebrated in our neighborhood on each of nine nights before Christmas. Neighbors up and down Laredo Street turn out, carrying candles to light the way for a young woman dressed as Mary and a man as Joseph. The procession stops at each house along the street to knock on the door, and in sung dialogue, Mary and Joseph asked for *posar*, lodging. Each night they are denied—until the last, Christmas Eve. My family participated every year at the King Ranch and in Laredito ever since we arrived here. Being part of las Posadas was difficult for chili stand families because of our nightly work on the plaza. But we did not open our stand on Christmas Eve. This year, our house would be the last visited—the one that granted lodging and invited everyone in for a fiesta. Our neighbors would bring pastries, candies, the makings of hot chocolate, and other treats. We would provide tamales. To feed everyone, our Tamalada needed to produce dozens of the tasty cornhusk-wrapped stuffed masa. They took hours to make. Preparations were easier and more fun with many willing hands.

"Well?" Antonio held out his open palms, then made a fist with one hand and thumbed his chest.

"Friends are always welcome to help."

"I hope that you think of me as more than a friend."

"You are one of my very best friends."

His smile faded. I had to be honest. I felt nothing more for him.

Ten days before Christmas Eve, Josefa still had no news. All she knew was that Papá was making a plan and he would tell us when he was ready. Despite her frequent bouts with nausea, Josefa looked as beautiful as ever, if a bit worried. But I doubted that anyone would guess her secret. Josefa's natural reserve served her well in times of secrecy.

Sunday afternoons were best for bringing many people together. So it was on a chilly but bright December Sunday afternoon that Elena, her mother, Mamá, Josefa, and I set up the tables in our adjoining yards. Josefa's job was to soak dozens of cornhusks. Elena and I were put to work pulling the tender pork that señora Hernández had cooked several hours with chopped onion, crushed garlic, and a bay leaf until the meat was so tender it almost fell apart. We seasoned the mountain of pork strips with salt, pepper, and some ground roasted chile piquin. I rendered lard in a pot with minced garlic, and Elena added the pork strips, mixing until well blended. Then I mixed in some Pérez chile sauce. The aroma made my mouth water.

While we were preparing the pork filling, Mamá beat lard until it was soft and creamy. To that she added *masa de maíz* mixed with baking powder and seasoned with salt. As Mamá blended the masa mixture into the lard, señora Hernández added small amounts of the pork broth until the mixture was a thick and creamy paste.

One of my older sisters brought a filling made with chicken. Another brought a sweet filling of dried fruits and nuts spiced with cinnamon and piloncillo, bound together with masa.

We laid out in sequence all the ingredients needed to make tamales. First came the soaked cornhusks. Next in line was a bowl full of masa paste. Then came a pan heaping with the pork mixture. Bowls of the chicken and the sweet filling waited in reserve until all the pork tamales had been made. Several tablespoons were placed beside each bowl so that two or three tamale makers could work simultaneously, on both sides of the table. We were ready.

Peter arrived at exactly the hour I had specified. Antonio showed up ten minutes later as my sisters and their husbands, my brothers and their wives, and my excited nieces and nephews filled the yard with laughter and chatter. The children's mothers went first, guiding little fingers through the various steps of tamale making.

After you went through the line, you stood your tamale on its folded end in a colander for steaming later, when the colander was full. Then, you went to the end of the line to begin another. Antonio was an old hand at this and moved quickly. But Peter had not made tamales before. So I took him through the process, step by step.

Josefa patted a soaked cornhusk between two towels for us. I stretched out the still moist husk in the palm of Peter's hand. "You open it like a fan with the broader end touching the tips of your fingers. Take a spoonful of the masa paste and spread it on the upper half of the cornhusk."

"Like this?" he said.

"Spread it more evenly."

He spread it too far.

"You do not want it to touch the ends of the cornhusk. We will fold those over later."

Peter scraped the masa away from the edges of his cornhusk. "Is this right?"

I inspected his work and nodded. "Now take a spoonful of the meat mixture and place it in the middle of the masa."

Peter did that easily in one try.

"¡Bueno! Now fold the edges of the cornhusk over, toward the center. This will keep the filling inside the husk."

He fumbled but got that done in two tries. His face brightened. "No need to say more," he said, and he folded the bottom of the cornhusk up and placed his finished tamale in the colander with the others. Peter waited for Mamá's assessment.

"¡Bravo!" Mamá said. "*Esa una buena.* That is a good one. You must make more." Her smile lit up her face as she patted his arm. Peter beamed.

We went through the line several more times and each time Peter made better-formed tamales. Mamá said that he was a big help. She put one batch in the pot to steam as the work went on until several dozen were made. These would be steamed, also, then packed and stored for Christmas Eve.

One of Papá's prized possessions was a used icebox he bought from a traveling peddler. It had suffered many dents and scrapes, but it still worked. On special occasions, he bought blocks of ice from the icehouse to place in its upper compartment. As the ice melted, the runoff was caught in a pan under the icebox that we collected and reused. We kept cooked tamales in the compartment below the ice until we needed to warm and serve them for the celebrations.

It had taken several hours of work but when done, the first batch of tamales was ready to eat and we were ready to eat them with seasoned rice and spicy beans and *atole.* My brothers told tall tales. Elena began to hum the Posadas melody, one her father had brought back from the mouth of the Río Grande where his parents lived. One by one, we picked up the refrain and together we sang:

"Las Posadas"
From Paredes, Américo. A Texas-Mexican Cancionero: Folksongs of the Lower Border. *Urbana-Champaign, Ill.: University of Illinois Press, 1976.*

Muy buenas noches,
aldeanos dichosos,
posada les piden
estos dos esposos.

Serán bandoleros
o querrán robar . . .

Robarte pretendo
pero el corazón
por eso en tu choza
pedí un rincón.

Vayan más delante,
está una pastoría,
que allí dan posada
de noche y de día.

Vegan, vegan, vegan,
Jesús y María
y su amado esposo
en su compañía.

Abranse esas puertas,
rómpanse esos velos,
que viene a posar
el Rey de los Cielos.

After a couple of rounds, Peter joined in, his baritone, like Papá's, complementing the tenors and the women's voices. He had a good ear for tone and for the language. When the singing drifted back to conversation, Papá held up his hand for quiet.

"I have good news. José has been on drives from the Río Grande to Kansas. He has a good-paying job as a horse wrangler on his boss's ranch in South Texas. And," he paused, accentuating our suspense, "he will be home for Christmas."

Cheers. Hoots. Whistles. Applause. The little children clapped.

"It will be good to see him again," I said to Peter.

"I wish I could. I will be with my family in Stonewall."

Atole

½ cup masa de maíz
5 cups water
5 tablespoons ground piloncillo
1 tablespoon ground cinnamon
1 teaspoon vanilla extract
Yield: 5 cups

Grate or slice the piloncillo cone until you have the desired quantity of sugar grains. Mix the piloncillo with the masa and the cinnamon. Heat the mixture until it just begins to boil, then reduce the heat and stir until well blended. Whisk the mixture with a molinillo.* The liquid should be smooth and moderately thick, without clumps. Blend in vanilla. Pour into cups. Serve hot.

*A wire kitchen whisk may be substituted for a molinillo.

"Of course." I was disappointed. "José will miss seeing you."

"I will be leaving in a few days. Mr. Kotula has given me a holiday. I will not return until after New Year's Day. I will leave this. It is my Christmas gift to you. Open it when your family exchanges gifts."

He handed me a small package wrapped in brown paper and tied with string.

"A book?"

"Not one to read, but one you need."

CHAPTER *20*

My family exchanged presents on January 6, the Epiphany, when the three kings bearing gifts for the baby Jesus arrived in Bethlehem. All through the holidays, I handled the package Peter had left with me, wondering what type of book he thought I needed. Many times, I was tempted to peek under the wrapping. Peter did not have to wait as long to open my present. His family shared gifts on Christmas Eve. I hoped that he liked the white handkerchief bearing his initials in one corner. It had taken me a long time to embroider them with a thread the color of his eyes.

When the Epiphany finally arrived, I kept his until last. From Elena, there were colorful ribbons for my hair. Señor and señora Hernández gave everyone two pecan pralines wrapped in a paper tied with a strand of yarn. From Mamá and Papá I received a length of linen lawn, and from Josefa, delicately drawn thread work at one end of the fabric. "You can make yourself a new chemise," they told me.

To each of the men, I gave bandanas I had cut and sewn from absorbent cotton cloth. In the heat of summer, they wrapped them around their heads to catch sweat before it dripped into their eyes. During hard labor, wet bandanas tied around their necks were cooling. They also made good masks to protect against dust raised by strong, swirling winds. The men were glad to get them.

This year, my misfortune benefited Mamá, señora Hernández, Elena, and Josefa. I gave each one of the rebozos I could not sell. Elena got the red and green one with the tassels that she favored. To Mamá, who liked bright colors, went the deep orange and blue one. Señora Hernandez was pleased with the violet and lime-green cotton. And to Josefa, I gave the black wool rebozo with its red, gold, and aqua threads. "To carry your baby," I whispered in her ear.

Antonio made his gifts at the forge. His Christmas gift to me was a ladle with a long handle. I owed Antonio for the rebozos, but he had not pressed me about that.

When it came time to open Peter's gift, everyone crowded around me. The string fell away with one tug at the neatly tied bow. I peeled back the wrapping paper.

"A book. What is it about?" Elena asked.

"Accounts." I flipped through the empty ruled pages. Tucked in the middle, where the pages were stitched together, was a twice-folded note:

Dear Lupe,
This will help you keep track of your business expenses. I wish you abundant prof-
its. ¡Feliz Navidad!
Peter

No one said anything. They turned away without comment. How could they understand? They had not been party to my conversations with Peter. I treasured my account book and blessed him for so thoughtful and useful a present.

We closed the chili stand early on an especially cold, wet, and windy week-night in mid-January. The plaza was virtually deserted. Once back home, Mamá, Papá, Josefa, and I sat around the fireplace wrapped in our warmest garments and blankets, sipping hot chocolate. I saw Mamá nod to Papá.

"*Esta es una buena oportunidad para hablar*," he began. "I have made ar-rangements with your *padrina* and *padrino*, your godmother and godfather, on the King Ranch." He was looking at Josefa. "They will provide you with a home until the birth of your child. Then we will see what we need to do. In a week's time, Mamá and I will travel with you to Santa Gertrudis to help you get settled there."

"Papá, *¿tengo que ir tan lejos?* Must I go so far away?"

"Sí, Josefa. I know of no other place where you would be as well cared for."

"And if Tomás returns?"

"I thought he did not know when that might be."

"He did not."

"Do you have a way to reach him?"

Josefa shook her head.

"We cannot wait for him, Josefa. We must think of the well-being of you and the child."

"The ranch is so far away."

"Do you know of a better place? Your Mamá and I want to protect you. This is the best way we know to do that."

Papá turned to me. "Lupe, we will expect you to take care of the chili stand. You will keep our house while we are away. Señor and señora Hernández and Elena will help you. Your older sisters and brothers will look in on you every day. You will spend the nights in the Hernández home."

Josefa started to speak, but Papá waved his hand. "*Ya está arreglado.* It is settled, Josefa."

That night I wrapped my arms around Josefa's trembling body.

"Papá has decided, Josefa. He will not change his mind."

"I do not want to be so far away. When Tomás returns, how will he find me? I know that Papá will not tell him where I am."

"We do not know if he will return, Josefa."

"He said he would."

I held her close.

"Will you make me a promise?" Her words were muffled against my shoulder.

"What do you wish?"

"When Tomás comes back, promise me you will tell him where I am."

"Defy Papá?"

"Pápa does not understand how much I love Tomás, Lupe. No other man could ever mean as much to me."

"But he did not give you an address or any way to reach him."

"Because he did not know where he would be staying."

"He could have sent you a letter."

"He must be busy, Lupe."

"What is the harm in your spending your confinement at the King Ranch? That will save you embarrassment here."

"I fear that my godparents will arrange a match. I will have to marry a man I do not love."

"Oh, Josefa. Do not borrow trouble. Take one step at a time."

"Promise me, Lupe."

I hesitated. I did not want to act against Papá's wishes.

"Please."

I offered a compromise. "If Tom O'Malley returns and asks me your whereabouts, I will tell him that Papá made arrangements for you and suggest that he talk with Pápa about his intentions. If he pledges marriage, I think that Papá will be satisfied."

"And you will let me know?"

"Yes, Josefa. I will send you word."

Josefa wiped her tears and sighed. "Thank you, Lupita. You are a good sister." I felt her body relax and moments later she was asleep.

They were en route south the following week. I would miss Josefa. My thoughts were troubled. *What if Tom O'Malley returned looking for her? Papá was unlikely to tell him where to find Josefa. Should I tell him about the baby? Should I give him clues to find her? What would he do? If Josefa saw him again, would it just bring her more heartache?*

That evening, I opened the chili stand with Elena and her parents. Señor Hernández helped us set up. Señora Hernández did the cooking. Elena served. And I entertained the patrons. I was telling about a pet rooster that Papá had on a trail drive when I saw Antonio take a seat on the bench to my left.

"Every morning, el Gallo would crow loudly, but he never got a response," I told my audience.

"Too far away from hens," a laughing patron said.

I nodded. "The closest ranch was over two hundred miles away. The Indians were astonished to see a rooster so far from a settlement. It was his habit to roost on the wagon hounds. One stormy night, he was blown off. There he hung under the wagon, upside down by one foot, all night long. Miguel found him the next morning. When he cut el Gallo free, Jesse said he looked and acted like he had been drinking hard liquor all night."

"Was he all right?" one of the women asked.

"Oh, yes. He was tenderly cared for by all the trail hands and the cook. It was not long before he was his bright self again. He made many long trips with Miguel, and was a source of pleasure and amusement for the entire camp."

I was about to begin a tale of a horse stampede when Antonio called my name. "Lupe."

I turned to face him. "¿Sí?"

"I would like to talk to you. Alone."

"You have a secret?"

"I have something I want to ask you."

"I can take care of the stand," Elena said.

I squeezed her arm and walked around the U-shaped tables to where Antonio now stood. He slung his guitar over his shoulder and led me to a bench near San Fernando Cathedral, not far from our stand but away from the hubbub on the plaza. It was chilly, and I pulled my rebozo around my shoulders. Antonio sat next to me. He looked at me with an intense expression. I didn't know what he was about to say but I felt the weight of it in his eyes.

He pulled his guitar forward, strummed a few chords, and began to sing a sad Spanish ballad about his deeply felt love for a beautiful brown girl, love unmatched by any other man in the world

I was touched, but not surprised.

"I have been thinking," he began. "It is time for me to start my own family."

I anticipated what he was about to say and steadied myself.

"I have spoken to your Papá. He has given his permission if you are willing." He shifted his guitar to his back, slid off the bench, knelt before me, and took my hand in his. "I would like you to be my wife, Lupe."

I was slow to respond, and he looked at me quizzically.

"Your proposal touches my heart, Antonio. I am honored. But I am not yet ready to marry."

He dropped my hand and returned to his seat on the bench. "Why not? You are old enough."

"Because I want to see if I can build our business."

"You can do that as a married woman."

"Antonio, making a home we would share, taking care of you, having and raising children—all that would use up my energies."

He rose. I looked up. I had not wanted to hurt him, but the look in his eyes told me that I had.

"I think there is another reason," he said. "You have feelings for Peter Meyer."

I did not want to admit that to Antonio.

"Can we wait for a while?" I asked.

"Lupe, I have a young man's needs. It is time that I found a wife. I cannot wait for long."

"You must do what is best for you."

"Trigueña Hermosa"
From Paredes, Américo. A Texas-Mexican Cancionero: Folksongs of the Lower Border. *Urbana-Champaign, Ill.: University of Illinois Press, 1976.*

"Then your answer is definite?"

I nodded. "That may be best." I did not say more. I had warm feelings for Antonio. I liked him as a close friend. But I did not love him in a romantic way. He escorted me back to the stand and abruptly left. I watched his receding back, shoulders slumped, head low. Antonio was right. I had special feelings for Peter. He understood my dreams. He had like dreams of his own. I cherished the thought of perhaps, one day, sharing my life with him.

The next time Peter came by the stand, I asked him to help me with the accounts ledger and offered him lunch at the Hernández home. He arranged with Mr. Kotula to be away from the store for an hour at midday on a Tuesday. After a meal of chiles rellenos, tortillas, and coffee, Elena, her parents, and I gathered around the table with Peter and the ledger.

"See here." I drew a line with my finger down the costs I had listed for all ingredients we used for our business. "Mamá and Papá have helped me itemize all our costs over the past two weeks, since New Year's Day."

"Very good," Peter said. "Assuming that your costs are not exactly the same every week, we need to work on monthly figures. Because you do not have that many weeks recorded yet, we can estimate using these figures—but it will be just an estimate. You understand?"

We all nodded.

"Now, we need to know how much you took in. Those figures are not here. Do you have them?"

I looked at Elena. "Do we know how much money we took in?"

"I gave all the money I had except my tips to your Papá before your parents left. But I have what I collected for the last two days." Elena pulled out the shallow wooden box we used to collect payment. Papá had made partitions for bills and coins of different denominations. It came in handy for making change. Elena counted the contents and reported. "We have five dollars seventy-five for two nights."

"My guess is that your profit may only be around two dollars a night," Peter said. "But that's a very rough estimate. We need more exact figures over a longer period of time. It will be helpful if you record what your patrons order, so that we'll know how much of each ingredient you should buy. Without that information, you could be wasting money on ingredients you don't need."

"We have to make enough to employ señora Hernández and Elena. Right now, all we can do is share some of what we collect in our cash box with them. But this is imprecise."

Peter shook his head. "It's bad business."

"I know. And I owe Antonio for the rebozos that did not sell."

"Do not despair, Lupe. I will help you balance the books. Just write down everything you spend for the business, every penny you collect from your customers, and the number and type of meals and drinks you serve. In a few weeks, we will have a better sense of what it will take to make your business profitable."

I learned about her on a Sunday afternoon in February, after Mamá and Papá had returned from the Wild Horse Desert. I remember my surprise and delight at seeing Peter at our front door. The day was sunny and pleasant, so I invited him into the yard. I offered him hot chocolate at our table.

"I have more figures about costs and sales," I told him. I assumed that he had come to help with the accounts.

"That is not why I am here, Lupe."

A long and uncomfortable silence followed. Our conversation was usually easy. I did not understand.

"Lupe, I have something I must tell you."

I put down my cup, looked directly into his eyes and nodded.

Peter swallowed hard, "Lupe, I had hoped that something might develop between us."

"I thought that was happening," I said.

"I had plans," he said, "for my future . . . that included you."

Then he spoke a name, "Katarina Behrens."

I shook my head. It was not one I knew.

"Katarina has just arrived from Prussia." Again, he swallowed. "She is from a family that knows my parents. She has come to settle in Stonewall. For now, she is staying with my aunt and uncle—on their farm. Her traveling companions are staying at my parents' home."

"For now?"

"Yes." Peter paused, then blurted out so quickly that I had to ask him to repeat himself, "She will move to my parents' home after we are married."

I felt as if I had been punched in the stomach.

Peter took both my hands in his. "Lupe, I did not want this. Please believe me. I did not want this to happen."

I felt a fog of confusion settle over me. I wanted to express the depth of my feelings for Peter but could not speak the words.

He continued to explain, "My parents made this match. They believe they are looking after my welfare. I cannot violate their trust in me."

"Peter," I whispered. "Did they do this because I am a Mexican girl?"

"No," he said.

"Are you sure?"

"They have not even met you."

"Have you told them about me?"

"Of course."

"Well?"

He paused and squeezed my hands before letting them go. "Lupe, I do not know."

CHAPTER *21*

I lay awake at night thinking of him. He dominated my dreams, and when I woke he was still heavy on my mind. I would rush by Mr. Kotula's store to avoid seeing him, although I yearned to. I wondered if I would ever be able to enjoy San Pedro Springs Park again. Memories of him were in all the places we had been together. I knew by the way Peter had delivered his news that he would not waver from his family's expectations. There was no hope for us. I had to accept his decision and not pine for him. It felt like the hardest thing I had ever been asked to do.

I continued to use the ledger, recording daily expenses and income. The little book was a tangible reminder of Peter, his note still tucked between its blank pages. I had sweet memories of our times together. But now, they were sad.

Mamá found me in one of those moments.

"¿Qué te pasa?"

"No es nada, Mamá."

She put one hand under my chin to raise my face and wiped away a tear with the other.

"I think it must be something. An affair of the heart, perhaps?"

Her expression was soft and kind and inviting. And then she opened the gates. "This is about Peter?"

Now the tears would not be held and the sobs came, deep, pent-up grief over my loss. Mamá took me into her arms and rocked me. Behind the purged frustration came a wave of sorrow, and then calm. Mamá handed me a cloth to wipe my eyes and nose. We sat facing one another and she said, "*Díme.*"

I recounted what Peter had told me about Katarina.

Mamá sighed. "It was to be expected, Lupe. Look at the contrast. Peter is Lutheran. You are Catholic. His family celebrates German traditions. Your heritage is Mexican. His parents are landowners and cotton farmers with a profitable farm. Your papá is a day laborer. We run a chili stand. They have more than we ever will. We live in different worlds."

"But I would be a good wife for Peter."

"The Meyers are not sure of that. There are too many bridges to build between our family and theirs. They see their son making a poor marriage if he were to wed you, a loss of status and no financial gain."

"But not for long. I can turn a good profit at our chili stand. I just need to find a way."

Mamá smoothed my hair. "They cannot be sure of that."

"The Meyers are not being fair, Mamá. They have not even met me."

"Did you ever wonder why Peter never brought his parents to our chili stand?"

"It is a long trip from Stonewall to San Antonio. It is difficult to be away for several days from the daily chores of caring for livestock and a sown crop."

"In fairness to Peter," Mamá said, "he had not asked Papá for your hand. Did he ever speak of marriage to you?"

"He did not propose formally. But he did talk about a life together for us."

"Lupe, many a young woman has her heart broken once or twice before she finds the right one. You may never completely forget Peter. You will be sad for a while. You may even find that your feelings turn to anger."

"Anger?"

"You are frustrated because you are being denied your most romantic dream. You may get mad at Peter for leaving you for another. But that too will pass, and the longing you feel will soften with time."

"My feelings for him are strong, Mamá."

"The hurt will go away. You will find a new love. Then Peter will become a faint memory."

"I hope so, Mamá. I cannot bear this pain for long."

"Trust me."

I clung to my comforting mother with her protective arms around me. She whispered in my ear, "The best way to forget is to stop thinking about him. Think, instead, about your work, Lupe. How are you going to make our chili stand profitable?"

That night, following Mamá's advice, I threw myself into entertaining our patrons with another of Papá's stories:

"Horse herds at the King Ranch number in the thousands. And hundreds have been trailed to Dodge City by way of San Antonio, Kerrville, and points north to the Red River. Miguel rode as head horse wrangler on a three-month drive to Kansas. One night, the hands turned the horses loose on tableland and made camp. Rain had been in the wind all day, but nothing had developed—until dusk. Spears of lightning were punctuated by rolling thunder. The time between lightning flash and thunderclap rapidly shortened. Miguel drove an iron picket pin into the ground, sinking it firmly, and tethered his horse to its end loop."

I paused so Elena could take orders from new arrivals. I counted fifteen in all. Most were cowboys here for a night on the town. With Mamá now back and señora Hernández making tortillas, Elena served everyone quickly and efficiently. They seemed to like her sparkling personality, too. She earned good tips, generously sharing them with me. When I protested, she said, "Just until you have enough to repay Antonio. After that, I will keep my tips for myself."

"I know about stormy nights with herds," one of the men said as he wiped the remnants of a tortilla across his plate. "I could tell you a story or two."

I spread my arms, fluttering the rebozo's fringes. "I would like to hear them, señor—after I have told mine."

He smiled and nodded. I continued.

"The next clap of thunder erupted overhead, startling a small herd of deer browsing nearby. A large buck with antlers so immense that Miguel wondered how he held his head up sprang in front of the herd. That set the horses to rearing, jumping, and snorting. A stampede was on. Running full out, the horse herd passed close to the camp. The remuda horses trembled and groaned with fright, and took off with the herd."

"The hands had not hobbled their mounts," one of the cowboys guessed.

I nodded. "Miguel ran to his horse. But before he could mount, the animal caught the contagion of fright, pulled up his stake and galloped away with the others."

"Trailing the picket!" another said, shaking his head. "Trouble."

"On the end of that trailing rope the picket became a ricocheting spear, threatening to stab anything or anyone in its erratic path. When his horse circled round in blind frenzy, Miguel dove for the picket. He grasped its shaft, clasping both hands around it. He hung on bouncing and bumping for a hundred yards before he could slow and finally stop the frantic animal. He scrambled into the saddle to try to catch and turn the herd. But by this time, they had crossed a creek and the storm was growing in intensity. The remuda horses were not far off and still bunched together. Miguel spurred his own tired mount toward them, readying his lasso. He took aim and tossed. The loop cleared the lead mare's head, settling around her neck. He pulled up parallel to the mare and turned her toward camp. The others followed."

"Bein' dragged like that—it can kill ya'," a diner volunteered.

"To be sure, Miguel was scraped, bruised, cut, and bleeding. Though sore all over, the next morning he mounted with the other men to look for the lost herd. They found most, though not all. The others could have been miles away by then. They had to move on."

"What happened to the ones that got away?"

"On the very next trip over the same route, Miguel saw horses with the flying *W* King brand."

"Where?"

"With Indian ponies."

"Did he take them back?" a woman to my right asked.

"That is a story for another night. We should hear your stories." I motioned to the man who earlier had said that he had tales to tell. "Before we do, who would like another plate? A drink? Another tortilla? A praline? Señor Hernández has a tray of freshly made ones, with more Texas pecans than you can count. They are delicious with a cup of coffee or hot chocolate."

Two ordered another cup of coffee and a smoke. But with the end of my story, many diners left. A few more took their places and I invited the cowhand to share his experiences, then retold my story. Traffic was slow for the rest of the night.

Elena and I pored over the account book at the end of the week, making entries for every foodstuff bought and sold each day.

"Our enchiladas are the most popular dish," she said.

"That is because they are the least expensive."

"We sell chili, too, and lots of coffee."

I added up the totals. "We are coming out ahead, but not by much. Storytelling by itself does not make diners order more food."

"Some buy more drinks when you tell stories."

"If only I could charge for my stories, Elena. We have to do something that other stands are not doing."

"You know," Elena started tentatively, "one of the women asked me what else we sold."

"Well, we tried rebozos, and that did not work."

"I think she meant what else did we have to eat."

A bright light flashed before my eyes. The idea was right there in front of me all the time. I just had not seen it. I beamed at Elena. "Gracias, Elena. That is the answer."

"What is, Lupe?"

"We have to add to our menu some signature dishes, foods unique to us, that can only be bought at our stand, nowhere else. The dish has to change every night. That will bring the customers back time and time again. As long as there is something new and delicious to enjoy at our stand, they will return."

"What would that be?"

"I do not know yet. But it should use chiles. We need to find out what the other stands are selling."

"I can do that while you are telling a story. There is rarely an order to fill once everyone is settled and served. You hold everyone's attention. I will see what people are ordering at other stands. In a few days' time, I should be able to make a list."

Soon after Elena shared her list with me, we joined Mamá and señora Hernández having coffee at the table in our yard. We poured ourselves a cup and sat across from them.

Señora Hernández smiled at us. "¡Hola! ¿Qué pasa?"

I began, "We have talked many times about ways to increase our income at our chili stand. Well, Elena and I were sharing thoughts last week and she gave me an idea."

"¿Qué es tu idea?" Mamá asked.

"We need a signature dish—to bring customers back and to attract new ones. One that we can vary from day to day, unlike anything else on the plaza. We need something costing little to prepare and so tasty and appealing that we can sell it at double what it costs to make."

"What, besides chili, frijoles, enchiladas, and tortillas, is sold at the other stands?" señora Hernández asked.

Elena answered. "I went around the plaza to see what customers were ordering. In addition to what we serve, they ordered sopas, pucheros, and tamales."

"What is missing?" I asked.

They looked from one to the other, then to me.

I paused, then gave the answer. "Chiles. All of the dishes may be flavored with chiles and the sauces made from chiles, but none of the dishes has a chile as its main ingredient. In our signature dishes, the chile will be the star."

Their faces lit up. I continued, "So which chile should that be? It must be easy to find, abundant, and cheap."

Mamá needed no time to think about that. "Green anchos . . . poblanos . . ."

"Chiles rellenos. Roasted fresh poblanos are tasty when filled," señora Hernández said.

"And we can fill them with many different mixtures. What are some of those fillings?"

"*Arroz y frijoles.* Rice and beans."

"*Los garbanzos. Chícaros.* Chickpeas."

"*Pollo y arroz.* Chicken and rice."

"*Pasas, nueces y el arroz.* Raisins, nuts, and rice."

"*Verduras picadas cocidas como calabacín y berenjena.* Diced cooked vegetables like zucchini and eggplant."

"*Lentejas.* Lentils."

"*Queso blanco y queso añejo.* White and aged cheese."

"*Carnitas de cerdo.* Pulled pork."

"*Bistec cortado.* Chopped beefsteak."

"Those would be very different from what people coming to the plaza expect," Elena said.

"There is a problem," señora Hernández said. "Chiles rellenos are usually battered with egg and fried. That would be expensive to do and difficult to do on the plaza."

"We could grill them instead. No batter. Let the poblano speak for itself," I suggested.

"That makes it much easier to prepare ahead of time," Mamá said.

"Now, that opens up another possibility," señora Hernández added.

"There are many ways to make poblanos. I like them cooked in vinegar and stuffed with queso blanco."

Chiles en vinagre. Not many diners on the plaza would have tasted those. "Señora Hernández, may I write down your recipe?" I asked.

"If it is only for our use."

"*Claro.* Of course."

Elena went into her room and returned with a notebook, pen, and a bottle of ink. She set them in front of me at the kitchen table.

"These are from school. The pen and ink come in handy to make lists. Sometimes I write down the stories I hear you tell at the chili stand to practice my written English." She pushed them toward me. "Use these for the recipe, Lupe."

Past the first several pages of English practice exercises and summaries of my stories were blank ones. That is where I recorded señora Hernández's recipe. I titled it "*Unos Chiles.* Some Chiles."

Elena looked over my shoulder. "You have nice penmanship, Lupe. You should write more recipes in the book."

"Sí," señora Hernández said. "I can tell you how to make the chiles rellenos de chícharos. Write this down," she said. It was the second recipe I recorded that day.

Many others would follow, recorded in all the notebook's spaces, even above and below the recipes I had recorded earlier. My manuscript cookbook became a collection of what I learned from good cooks over time.

Writing the recipes made me think of other ways to prepare our foods.

"Mamá sometimes chops chiles into masa to make spicy tortillas. We could do that for our chili stand customers, too." Ideas were tumbling over one another now.

"Sí." Señora Hernández nodded her head vigorously. "Buena idea, Lupe. That would be a change from the tortillas everyone else on the plaza serves."

"We are just offering our customers some of the best of our cooking— the kind of food we enjoy at home."

Mamá clapped her hands. "*¿Cuándo empezamos?* When do we begin?"

Chiles en Vinagre
CHILES IN VINEGAR

Señora Hernandez suggested this variation on stuffed poblanos. She liked to soak the poblanos in vinegar before filling them with cheese. When señora Hernández dictated her recipe for them, she left out steps that an experienced cook would know. Here is her recipe as I recorded it. The English version gives additional directions.

6 poblano chiles
1 cup vinegar
1 teaspoon oregano
1 teaspoon salt
queso fresco
Yield: 6 servings

Chiles en Vinagre

Se pican los chiles con un alfiles y se van poniendo en alcol juego para una botella de vinagre un cuarto de aceite bueno, un pedacito de pilon-cillo, tomillo mejorana, laurel, oregano y un poquito del alcohol en que estuvieron los chiles, se les agrega ajos y cebolla saucodrados ponien dole sal suficiente a los 8 dias ya estan buenos. Para chiles grandes se abren y se desvenon y luego se pican.

Poblanos in Vinegar

Roast and peel the poblano chiles. Remove seed balls and veins but leave the stems attached if possible. Place the chiles in a pot and cover with vinegar. Add oregano and salt to taste. Cook over medium heat and bring to a simmer, but do not allow liquid to boil. Remove the chiles from the heat and let stand for 2-3 hours. After removing the chiles from the vinegar solution, pat each dry. Fill each chile with queso fresco. Grill until the cheese melts. Serve hot.

Variations

The poblanos in vinegar may be filled with some of the same mixtures we use with poblanos that have been roasted and peeled but not cooked in vinegar.

y un clavo, ó mas enteros, al gusto; y unas pasas, tambien á que hierban, con el almibar; asi que esté de un punto regular, se echan alli las patas, á que den un lijero hervor; luego se apartan, y se les echã; unas ojitas de laurel, y ajonjoli tostado por ensima; Se toman frias, pero es mejor tomarlas calientes, por la manteca, que tienen:.

Unos Chiles.

Se les quitan las semillas y benas, á los chiles verdes anchos; y se echan en vinagre fuerte con todo y rabo, y se le echá al vinagre, orégano, y sal; y se ponen en una olla, muy serca de la lumbre, no sentados en la lumbre, nomas á que les de el calor; se dejan, asi por dos, ó tres horas, y despues se sacan, del vinagre; y se rellenan de queso fresco, y asi se sirven.

Frituras.

Rebanadas de Butifaras, enbueltas en huevo vatido cortado y fritas criadillas de carnero, despues de cosidas, rebanadas, se frien en aseite, y despues enbuel-

Spanish Recipe for Chiles en Vinagre, Chiles in Vinegar, Pickled Poblanos
Cocina Mexicana [MS cookbook TX 715.M4 C6553 1880z], Rare Books Collection, University of Texas at San Antonio Libraries Special Collections, p. 125.

Se freirá en manteca sebolla, ajos, jitomates y chile berde gordo, todo picado; y lla rendido y con sal, se le agregá huevos, se mezclan, y cuando esten cuajados, se unta una cazuela con manteca, se pondrá una capa de huevos batidos, otra de pan tostado en manteca, otra de los huevos rebueltos, agregándole trositos de jamon, longaniza, chorisitos, huevo, todo cosido. alcaparras, aceitunas, pasas almendras, perejil picado, pichones cosidos y en cuartos, otra de rebanadas de pan, y así irán poniendose hasta concluir, entre una y otra, huevo batido, y polvo de pimienta, la última será de huevo batido, se pondrá á dos fuegos suaves, y cuando esté se le echará azúcar.

Tratado de Rellenos.

Chiles rellenos de Chícharos.

Azados los chiles berdes grandes, y estando pelados, desbenados y lavados, se rellenan con un reboltillo de chicharos cosidos, y rasonados, con sebolla, ajos y jito-

Chiles Rellenos de Chícharos
Cocina Mexicana [MS cookbook TX 715.M4 C6553 1880z], Rare Books Collection, University of Texas at San Antonio Libraries Special Collections, p. 97-98.

mates picados, menudos y frito en manteca, con
sal, clavos pimienta molida, y cuando esté rendido
el recaudo, se agregarán los chícharos, y huevos me-
dio batidos, y así que esté cuajado, y frio, se relle-
narán los chiles, se enbolveran en huevo batido, y
se freirán, y se echan en la salsa siguiente, bien
sazonada. Se freirá sebolla rebanada, ajos picados,
y jitomates crudos, clavos, pimienta y cominos, todo
molido, y estando se le agregá sal, harina dorada
en manteca, aseite vinagre, calabasitas rebanadas, ase-
itunas, y chilitos. Los que ban rellenos de queso, se
hasen en la misma disposision. Lomismo se hasen
los que ban rellenos de papas, cosidas picadas y fritas,
con pan, sal y pimienta, todo molido, y en cualqui-
era, de las salsas, que se quiera.

Calabasitas Rellenas.

Cosidas y quitadas las tripas, se rellenan con chorizon
y lomo picado, y frito, ó con queso fresco, ó con lechu-
gas, ó aselgas cosidas, picadas y esprimidas, y fritas,

CHAPTER 22

The very next day, Elena and I bought some poblanos from the produce vendors on the plaza. We selected them carefully for roasting—medium size, with dark skins and nice flat sides. The most time-consuming part was peeling their skins after roasting. But Mamá and señora Hernández gave us helpful tips.

"*Asen los chiles*. Roast the chiles. If they are roasted on the hot comal, their sides will blister well," Mamá told us. "They must blacken evenly. If any part is not touched by the heat, the skin will resist you."

"Place the hot roasted poblanos in a bowl and cover tightly with a towel. Let them steam for a while," señora Hernández said. "After they are cooled, you will be able to peel off the charred skins. Use the blade of a small knife to help strip away the resistant skins. Then, slit the chile down one side and cut out the seed ball just under the stem. Leave the stem in place. For very mild chiles, take out the veins, too. Rinse, and your pepper will be ready. "

We decided that our first signature poblano dish would be a mixture of softened, mashed garbanzo beans fried with finely chopped onion, garlic, and fresh tomatoes, and seasoned with cumin, salt, and pepper. We stuffed the peppers with the chickpea mixture, and layered them on a platter Mamá covered with a towel. We carried this with our regular supplies to the chili stand that night.

Our very first customers were a tourist and his wife, both new to San Antonio. They looked around the plaza, wide-eyed. I called them over and said, "Have you ever tasted grilled chile relleno?"

"No, ma'am," the husband said. "We have no experience with food

Chile Relleno de Chícharos
POBLANO STUFFED WITH CHICKPEAS

4 medium flat-sided poblanos
1 cup dried chickpeas*
1 small onion, finely chopped
1 clove garlic, minced
1 tomato, finely chopped
1 teaspoon cumin
1 teaspoon each salt and pepper, according to taste
½ cup water
queso blanco (optional)
Yield: 4 servings

This recipe is for four servings. We prepared dozens to serve at the chili stand by filling them ahead of time and grilling the chile relleno for each order.

Roast the poblanos in an oiled pan over medium heat, turning until all sides are well blistered. It will be difficult to peel off skin unless the whole surface of the chile is blistered. Wrinkles or folds in the poblano make it hard to roast the pepper evenly; if the poblanos have smooth, flat sides, roasting will be easy. If a chile won't lie flat, press lightly with a spoon to make contact with the hot pan.

Place roasted chiles in a bowl and cover tightly** to allow them to steam for about 20 minutes, or until cool. Mamá always warned us to be careful when handling even mildly hot chiles, like poblanos, and especially to avoid touching your eyes, lips, or nose.

After steaming in the bowl, peel the skins from the chiles. If well charred, the skins should come off easily. Use the blade of a knife to gently scrape off the more resistant skins. The skins at the cap of the chile around the stem may not give way, as they rarely come into direct contact with the pan's hot surface and do not char. But my customers did not eat the chile's cap, leaving it on their plates with the stem still attached.

Cut a slit down the length of each chile and cut out the ball of seeds, leaving the stem in place. If you remove all seeds and veins, the chile will be mild. If you want a little heat, leave the veins in place.

Prepare the chickpea filling by first washing the dried chickpeas and soaking them in hot water for an hour. Then simmer in a saucepan filled with water for 2 hours. When the chickpeas are soft, drain and mash them to a pulp. We did this in a molcajete.***

Coat a pan with lard or oil. Fry finely chopped garlic and onion until the onion is soft. Add the mashed chickpeas and chopped fresh tomatoes with ½ cup water. Season with cumin, salt, and ground black pepper. Cook until the liquid has evaporated and the filling is firm. Add more water if it evaporates before all ingredients have mixed well. Fill the roasted chiles with the chickpea mixture. You may add queso blanco if you like the texture of melted cheese with the chickpea mixture. The stuffing will peek out of the chile.

When ready to serve, grill the chiles on a comal or griddle until the chile and the filling are heated through. Then ladle some heated chile sauce over the stuffed poblano, according to taste. Serve with grilled tortillas.

Other stuffings may be used with the poblanos before they are grilled.. We sometimes substituted cooked rice or mashed lentils for the chickpeas, adding them with chopped tomato and spices to the fried onion and garlic, with just enough water to keep the mixture moist but firm. We used beans in the same way, mashing them before adding them to the tomatoes, then to the onion, garlic, and spices.

Fresh vegetables in season make tasty fillings, too. We added cooked and diced zucchini or summer squash, eggplant, corn kernels, beets, and carrots to fried onions, garlic, cumin, salt, and pepper, then stuffed the vegetable mixture into the poblanos before grilling. Sometimes we added cheese such as queso fresco, queso añejo or queso blanco—whatever we could find in the market.

Variations

For sweet poblanos, we used rice mixed with raisins and nuts, seasoned with cinnamon, and sweetened with piloncillo. We usually made a syrup by melting the ground or chipped piloncillo in warm water, then added tablespoons of the syrup to the rice, raisin, and nut mixture until it was sweetened to taste.

For special occasions, we pulled chicken and pork that had been slow-cooked for several hours in a dutch oven until tender. For added flavor, we would brown the meat in some lard or oil before adding water to the meat in the dutch oven. After the meat was thoroughly cooked, we pulled it apart with a fork or our fingers and added it to the fried onions, garlic, and tomato. Sometimes we fried ground or chopped beefsteak and mixed it with the onion and garlic, adding cheese just before grilling. There were seemingly unlimited possibilities for changing the taste of the chile relleno by mixing different ingredients and, especially, by using various spices.

We always ladled our chile sauce over the grilled stuffed poblano unless customers preferred a milder taste.

The chile relleno became our signature dish because we could vary the filling from night to night to surprise our customers and keep them coming back for more.

Canned chickpeas may be used instead of the dried form. They will need only to be mashed before heating.
** *Plastic wrap may be used to seal the bowl of roasted poblanos.*
*** *A food processor may be used instead of a molcajete.*

from these parts. I came to try something spicy hot."

"Then you are in for a treat. For only fifteen cents a plate, I can offer you a delicious chile filled with tasty morsels, and chile tortillas, too."

"That sounds good. Bring a plate for each of us."

The woman put her hand on her husband's arm. "I don't want my mouth to burn."

"Señora, our poblanos are mild. I will not put hot sauce on yours, and we will make plain tortillas for you."

I called the order to Mamá and she and señora Hernández grilled the stuffed poblanos on the hot comal. They prepared one with our chile sauce and one without, added tortillas, with and without chiles, and Elena served the couple.

I watched the man slice his fork through the sauce and chile, scoop a piece with its filling onto his fork and into his mouth. His wife watched his face before touching her own meal. I held my breath. He chewed, savored, and swallowed. "This is delicious, señorita. I have never tasted anything like it."

He turned to his wife. "Go ahead," he said, motioning to his wife's plate. "Try the chile . . . what did you call it?" he asked me.

"Chile relleno—grilled chile relleno."

The woman tentatively cut a very small piece of her poblano and tasted it.

When she smiled, I knew that we were fine.

"Perhaps you would like some coffee?" I asked. The man nodded.

While they were eating, a couple of passersby caught sight of the poblanos with their fillings spilling out onto the plates. They stopped to peek over the diners' shoulders.

"Those look good. How much?"

Elena responded, "Fifteen cents for a chile relleno and tortilla."

"I can get a meal for a dime at other stands."

Elena looked at me.

"We have enchiladas for five cents and chili for ten, just like all the other stands. But you will not get a chile relleno anywhere else on the plaza. They cost more to prepare. Ours are a bargain at fifteen."

"Then I must try one. I'll take a plate," he said, throwing one long leg after the other over the bench. He tugged at his companion's arm. "Do you want one?"

"Sure looks good. One for me, too, por favor."

Before the first couple left, they told me how much they had enjoyed their meal. "Tell everyone you meet," I said, "that the Pérez chili stand just behind San Fernando Church has a signature dish that is like no other."

Our satisfied customer nodded and thanked me again. He must have talked to many because soon we had a steady stream of customers asking for "the stuffed chile." In two hours, we had sold every poblano we had brought. Disappointed customers had to be turned away with "Come back tomorrow. We will have more." On the chiles rellenos alone, we had doubled our money.

The next night, we brought twice the number of poblanos. We sold out of chiles rellenos but kept turning out the chile tortillas to make enchiladas, to serve with chile, or to sell separately for a penny apiece. Curious patrons of other stands stopped by just to sample our tortillas. Word was traveling fast. Our profits were improving nightly. We were all energized by our success. I was so engaged with food that thoughts of Peter were few and fleeting—until he appeared at our stand.

"You look surprised to see me," he said.

"I am." I felt stiff and awkward.

"I had hoped to see you at the store, but Mr. Kotula said that you came for your supplies when I was away for my lunch."

"I thought it best that way."

"You won't have to time your shopping to my schedule anymore."

I had avoided eye contact until now.

"My father has called me back to the farm. One of my brothers broke a leg and cannot work the land. Papa is short handed. He needs me to help. I must go."

"When will you leave?"

"Tomorrow. This means that I must abandon my dream of store ownership. At least, for now."

"I am sorry, Peter. I wish I could help you."

"I know you do, Lupe." He stood tall. He was quiet for a moment, his eyes holding mine in a gaze I would long remember. "But you . . . you appear to be doing well." He glanced over the diners digging into chiles rellenos and calling for more chile tortillas and coffee.

"I have to help Elena," I said, but he seemed not to hear me.

"Your dream is coming to pass, Lupe. ¡Buena suerte!" He turned and walked away. For the last time, I watched Peter's rangy strides take him away from me and felt anew a pang of regret.

"Lupe," Elena called. "We have new customers, more than I can handle."

I turned to the newcomers, swallowed my heartache, and in a cheerful voice said, "We have tasty chiles rellenos and chile tortillas. Would you like some?" But my insides hurt.

Elena was a good companion. She lifted me up. I do not remember her ever expressing a negative thought about anyone, about anything. She found joy in life wherever she could. Although I did not confide in her, she helped me concentrate on making our signature dishes. Together, we became skilled at roasting and peeling the chiles. Each day we turned out increasing numbers of poblanos, ready to be stuffed. And early each morning, when the produce vendors arrived on the plaza, we walked from stand to stand, taking stock of their produce. As early buyers, we got the best, filling our baskets with vegetables in season. Back home, after we slept, the four of us decided together how we would use the fresh vegetables to make stuffing for the poblanos. We would chop them, always a mix of texture, flavor, and color, and fry them with onion and garlic, salt and pepper, adding a spice from our rack of cumin, oregano, cinnamon, cloves, anise, and, of course, chiles, to complement their tastes. On Saturdays, we added chopped beefsteak.

With Papá and señor Hernández, we sampled our signature recipe of the day. Each of us would give our view. We frequently improved the recipes during these trials. Our chile relleno dishes succeeded in attracting more customers. The nightly change of fillings brought diners back time and time again. Now successful, I was enjoying my work, although I missed Josefa—and Peter.

In rational moments, I reminded myself that Peter was compelled by family loyalty and parental decree. There was little I could do to bring him back. He had made his choice. I pushed him far back into the deep recesses of my mind. Now and then, he invaded my dreams. But on awakening, I willed him away and concentrated on our menu.

During one of our taste tests, Papá took an envelope from his shirt pocket. He pulled from it a paper folded in fourths. I could see a scrawl of handwriting. The author had used a blunt pencil and the letters were thick and large, their message in Spanish.

"*Tengo buenas noticias del rancho King.* I have good news from the King Ranch," he said.

"Josefa?" I asked.

"*Sí. Esta carta es de su padrino.* This letter is from her godfather. He says that he has made a match for Josefa with one of the vaqueros at the ranch. Gilberto Gonzalez is his name. He is a little older than Josefa, a widower, but without children. He is well regarded among the people there. He will make a good home for Josefa."

"*¿Cómo le parece eso a Josefa?* How does Josefa feel about that?" I asked.

"*Está agradecida.* She is grateful." The expression in Papá's eyes told me not to probe any further.

But I wanted to know more. "I mean, Papá, does she love him?"

"Love has to be earned, Lupe. A marriage should not be based on infatuation. Life is not a romance. This is a good match."

"Why did Josefa move so far away?" señora Hernández asked.

I blinked back tears and hoped no one would see.

"We used to live there," Papá answered.

"What brought you here?" The question was from señor Hernández.

"I could not work horses and cattle after my injury."

"Captain King would have given you another job, Jorge." Mamá said.

Papá gave Mamá the same look he had given me. "I thought it best to move."

"I did not think that Josefa was homesick for the King Ranch. She never mentioned it. She seemed happy here. Such a beautiful girl," señora Hernández said. "I saw how the young men looked at her on the plaza. And that actor—what was his name—seemed smitten with her."

"Perhaps she is too beautiful," Papá said. "But now she will soon be a married woman in her own home where she can raise a family. We should celebrate that."

Papá brought out a jug of pulque and four glasses. He poured some for Elena's parents, Mamá and himself.

"What about us?"

"This is too strong for you," Papá said. But he paused, holding the jug in midair. "Well, perhaps a sip," he said, and poured enough of the potent brew for one sip into each of our coffee cups.

"*También tenemos un anuncio alegre.* We have a happy announcement, also," señora Hernández said. "Elena, speak."

We all turned to the young woman with the dancing eyes and bouncing curls.

"This just happened," she said. She looked from one to the other and we stared back, waiting for the news. Elena seemed about to burst. "Antonio Ortiz has asked me to marry him."

"*¿Y qué le contestaste?* And what did you answer?" her mother prompted.

"Sí."

I rose and went to where Elena sat to embrace her. "I am happy for you both," I said.

"My marriage will not interfere with my work at your stand, Lupe. I have spoken with Antonio about that. He has no objection. You can count on me."

"Until the babies begin to arrive."

"By then, Lupe, you will have a thriving business with many people to wait on customers."

"I hope you are right."

"*Otro brindis.* Another toast," señor Hernández said.

Papá poured a little more pulque for each.

"Elena and Antonio."

After the Hernández family left, I asked Papá to share more about Josefa.

"Señor Gonzalez has agreed to give her child his name. It is better that Josefa is married when she delivers. Her padrinos cannot provide a home for her indefinitely. Josefa's husband will care for her and the child and she will not be disgraced. There is nothing more to say, Lupe."

"May I ask another question?"

"If it is not about Josefa."

"It is about us, about you. Why did you move our family to San Antonio when none of us wanted to leave the King Ranch?"

"When the time is right, I will tell you . . . on one condition."

"What is that?"

"You must keep it a secret while I am alive."

CHAPTER 23

"*Estás muy pensativa*. You are deep in thought, Lupe," Papa said as he sat down near me.

"I was going over our accounts."

"And? What have you found?"

I smiled at him. "Much to be happy about, Papá. We are making money. Each week, our income goes up a little more. Customers are returning, and they are bringing friends. Our chile relleno variations are the reason. Each night, we offer a different filling. Some customers return several times a week to be surprised by the contents of our poblanos. Antonio tells me that some make bets on what the next filling will be. And our increased business helps señor Hernández sell more of his candies."

"You should be dancing around the room. Instead, you seem unusually pensive."

I did not want Papá to know that I had been thinking about Peter. "I wonder if we will be able to meet demand for our chiles rellenos. We sell out every evening and have to turn people away. We make enough to pay señora Hernández and Elena for their work, but we are not yet in a position to hire more help."

"*Necesitamos conejos*. We need rabbits."

"Rabbits?"

"Yes, something that multiplies rapidly. But I did not come to talk about the business. I am ready to share with you my secret—provided you keep it."

I put down my pencil and closed the ledger, caressing its cover, and turned to face Papá. "Of course. I promise."

Papá sat opposite me and in just above a whisper, began:

"I was doing well on the King Ranch. I was head horse wrangler, respected for my horsemanship by all Kineños and Captain King alike. I could hold my own with even the youngest and most skilled. I was proud, Mamá was content, and our niños were happy. We were living *la buena vida*.

"In those days, Captain King often sent four or five thousand cattle north to market. He would sell the herd to a trail boss at Texas prices and cover *el jefe*'s expenses for salaries and provisions for the drive. After the cattle were sold, the difference between the Texas price and the sale price in Kansas was split between the trail boss and the captain.

"I had done many different jobs on more trail drives than I can count. My favorite was as head horse wrangler, taking care of the remuda and moving large horse herds north for sale. I was good with horses; I was good with cattle; and I could cook—an all 'round hand. So, when Mr. Stevens, one of the captain's trail bosses, needed an assistant for a drive of six thousand cattle, I got the job. Assistant to el jefe meant a nice bonus after the cattle were sold in Kansas."

"This is what I mean, Papá. You were doing very well. Why did you give that all up and leave?"

He raised his hand to quiet me and continued, "Yes, Lupe, I was respected. But then things changed.

"It happened near the Nueces River. We got the cattle bedded for the night and set up camp. This was a very large drive. Four of us had to guard at each shift. After dinner, I was in the saddle, riding around the herd, watching for any signs of trouble. I noticed some restlessness in heifers near some shadowy brush, but I could see no reason for their behavior. They settled down. I thought that whatever had upset them was no longer of concern and decided not to ride closer to check. That was my mistake. In a sudden burst, the herd broke—a stampede of thousands of cattle. Can you imagine it? Those restless heifers started it and the fright spread like wildfire through the herd.

"I put my horse in pursuit of the leaders. My fellow guards on duty that night joined up. Hearing the commotion, other hands jumped from their bedrolls, mounted their horses, and tried to turn around the mass of frantic cattle. We caught the leaders and threw them back to the tail end of the herd. But they broke again. We were catching, throwing back, and catching again until three in the morning. Finally, they quieted and we resumed guard duty. But I was worried, Lupe. I feared that we had lost many."

"What caused the stampede?"

"Something was in that brush. I could not be certain, but when I passed

I saw what I thought was the glint of eyes deep in the dark foliage. Whatever it was, it struck fear in the cattle." Papá shook his head, remembering.

"Stampedes happened all the time on the range. If not a menacing animal, lightning would get one going, or thunder, or gunshots. You told me that yourself."

Papá nodded. "But lurking predators can be handled.

"At first light, we took count. My fears were confirmed. Half the herd was missing. Half! Three thousand cattle. We fanned out looking for them. A couple of men retrieved a few stragglers. Some had broken legs and we had to put them down right where they had fallen. The others? Who knows? Maybe Indians got them. Maybe they just kept running for miles beyond our search area. Maybe they died. Wherever they went, they were gone from us.

"My carelessness caused Mr. Stevens the loss of half his money. Captain King also lost the sizeable profit that three thousand head would bring in Kansas—because of my bad judgment. I knew better. A good vaquero investigates every sign of restlessness in his animals. I had ignored one. And because of that, my bosses lost not an eighth or a quarter, but half of their investment. From that day forward, I could not look Captain King or Mr. Stevens in the eye."

"Pero, Papá, one mistake does not undo years of good and loyal service."

He reached out and stroked my cheek. "That was a big mistake. I was about to make another. I do not know, Lupe, if you can appreciate the pain of losing face like I did on that trail drive. I was so ashamed. I apologized to Mr. Stevens. 'Everyone's wages will be affected by this loss,' he said. That caused me to feel worse.

"We drove the remaining cattle to Kansas. All the way there and on the return trip, I lay awake at night remembering the stampede, wishing it had not happened, and worrying about how I would tell the captain."

"What happened when you got home?"

"I went to see the captain, told him the truth, and accepted blame. He was upset over the loss of so many cattle, but generous in his designation of fault. 'Every man on duty that night shares the responsibility,' he said. He also understood how this blot on my record affected me. 'I know you are troubled by this. It may be best for you to work on the ranch for a while until you regain your confidence.'

"I remember your mamá giving me the same advice. 'For as long as I have known you,' she said, 'you have been respected for your horsemanship. You are one of the best vaqueros on the ranch. Work with your beloved horse herd. You will soon find your strengths again.'

"I took courage from her. But luck had turned against me.

"My first day back with the King horse herd, I gained the trust of a young mustang in the corral. By morning's end, I had successfully saddled him. The next day, I was able to mount and we walked around the perimeter of the corral. He was behaving well, all collected and contained. He learned quickly and was unusually tractable for so young a colt. By the third day, he was walking comfortably under leg control. I eased him to a trot. He transitioned seamlessly. By week's end, again with leg and heel pressure alone, he began a canter, moving into the gait like he had been doing it all his life. I hardly touched rein. It was so easy that I decided to take him to the next level the very same day. I rarely moved so quickly with green horses. I rode him out of the corral. He was fine, so I set him walking, then into a trot, then a canter. We quickened the pace and for a moment I thought he was the best young colt I had ever trained.

"But I had moved him too fast. Without warning, he bucked, throwing me over his head. His kicks were strong and steady. He was too fast for me. Before I could roll away, he ran over me, striking my leg hard. It sounded like a rifle shot, the crack of bone. I tried to get up. But I could not stand. That is all I remember. I am told that I passed out. Friends carried me to the barn. When I revived, the doctor was setting my fractured and splintered leg. I would forever be crippled. You know the rest, Lupe."

"Did the captain fire you?"

"No, he said he would find something for me to do. But I could not accept."

"Horses are strong, spirited animals, Papá. Everyone knows that they are hazardous to work with, especially young untrained colts."

"Try to understand, Lupe. My poor judgment caused Captain King and Mr. Stevens the loss of three thousand head and then the loss of my labor. How could I stay and face the other men day after day, no longer able to do my share of the work?"

I reached out to take his hand. The calloused skin felt rough in mine. "You are a noble man, Papá." I held his palm to my cheek.

"Remember, Lupe, while I am alive you must tell no one about this. Promise again so I may be certain."

"*Te lo prometeré*. I promise you, Papá."

"We need rabbits." Papá's comment kept coming to mind. *What "rabbit" could I make?*

It came to me while watching Mamá prepare the masa for chile tortillas. We always made the masa at home, then carried it to the plaza where Mamá, and now señora Hernández, too, patted balls of dough into tortillas they grilled on the comal.

"Mamá," I said, "*¿Vas a hacer una tortilla para mí?* Will you make a tortilla for me? One with chiles?"

"*¿Tienes hambre?* Are you hungry?"

"No, I will not eat it. I have an idea. Please, Mamá, lightly grill one for me."

Mamá patted out the masa, added finely chopped chiles, and grilled the tortilla. When she gave it to me, I placed it on a clean tile we used as a cutting board. I examined the thin patty, a near-perfect circle about five inches in diameter and an eighth of an inch thick. Mamá was a master tortilla maker. "We are going to make chips de chile tortillas."

With a small knife, I cut the tortilla into quarters.

"Aha!" Mamá said. She rendered lard in her frying pan and deep fried the triangles until they began to bubble up and turn golden brown and crispy on both sides. She placed them on a towel to drain. We sprinkled them with salt and each of us sampled one. Mamá smiled. "I think I will have another."

"Me too. We can sell them as chile chips."

We spent the rest of the afternoon preparing batches of chile chips. Señora and señor Hernández, Elena, and Papá all agreed. "Delicioso."

Elena and I introduced chile chips to our customers by giving free samples. Peter had told me that when Mr. Kotula introduced a foodstuff in his store, he gave away small samples and kept a record of how many customers purchased the product. If few did, he did not restock. If many purchased the item, that spelled profit. And he added it to his inventory.

We offered one free chile chip to each customer, and set the price at eight, the equivalent of two tortillas, for two cents. By the end of the first week, we were selling out every night. We had found our rabbits.

CHAPTER 24

Josefa's baby came the following spring. Papá read her letter to Mamá and me.

My Dear Parents and Sister,
He is here. My baby boy arrived at 2 a.m. on the first of June. We are both well. Gilberto is happy to have a son. We will christen the baby in a few weeks at the church in town. Gilberto's family and my godparents are making arrangements for the celebration. I wish that you could attend, but I know it is a long trip. I am hopeful that you can meet your new grandson and nephew soon. I miss you all very much.
Con cariño,
Josefa

"*¿Podemos visitarla, Papá?* Can we visit her, Papá?" I asked.

He shook his head. "*Esto no es un buen momento.* This is not a good time. We would have to shut down our stand for too long, Lupe. We may be forced to soon enough."

"What do you mean?"

"Word on the plaza is that it all vendors may have to leave."

"*¿Por qué?*"

"They say that a city hall will be built there."

"Is this true?"

Papá shrugged. "*No sé. Es un rumor.*"

After we had set up our stand and were waiting for our first diners of the evening, I sought out señor Hernández. The candy men were the plaza's informal messengers. With their portable candy trays, they moved about freely. They talked to lots of people in just about every section of the plaza. Vendors often paid them to carry messages to friends on the other side of the square. Señor Hernández usually stayed close to our chili stand in the evenings, selling candies for dessert to our diners. He also took his trade to other parts of the square when business at our stand slowed. Like other mobile vendors, he heard news first.

"*¿Has oído el rumor?* Have you heard the rumor?" I asked him.

He nodded. "*Cada día, hay un fragmento de noticias.* Every day, there is a snippet of news."

"When will we be pushed off?"

"When the cornerstone is laid."

"Is there a date?"

"Perhaps next year."

"Are you sure?"

"That is what I hear. I was told by the reporter from the *San Antonio Daily Express*, who is on the plaza often."

Qué mala suerte. What bad luck. Just when our chili stand is turning a profit, we have to close. The thought kept repeating in my head. After all that work, powers beyond our control will put us out of business. *¡Es injusto!* It is unfair! My frustration turned to anger. I was in no mood to tell a story, and my halfhearted attempt landed with a thud. My patrons did not complain, but I got no tips for storytelling that night. I could not have accepted any in good faith if they had been offered. I was awful. "Good thing we have an interesting poblano tonight," I said to Elena.

"What have you filled the poblanos with esta noche that makes them interesting?" The voice was Antonio's.

Elena answered him, "Would you like to find out?"

"Claro." Antonio sat on the bench, squared his shoulders and unrolled the napkin Elena had placed before him to find a fork and spoon. He made a fist around each, tilting them upright to demonstrate his readiness to eat. Elena went for his plate.

"Why so serious?" he asked me.

"Did you know that we—all the vendors—will have to close our stands?"

"¡No! ¿Por qué?"

"They say that the plaza has been chosen for a new city hall."

"¿Cuándo?"

"En un año. And just when we are beginning to turn a nice profit."

"There are other plazas." He began to name them. "Alamo, Washington, Milam, Zacatecas . . ."

"I know," I interrupted his list. "I have considered each, but there will never be another marketplace like Military Plaza. People from all walks of life and parts of the country—world even—come here, rub shoulders, converse, and enjoy our Mexican food."

"I see some of the same faces when I come to dine. It looks like you have a large number of loyal customers. Many would follow you to another place."

Elena returned with Antonio's plate. It contained a large pickled poblano, a double helping of frijoles, and three chile tortillas.

"*El sabor*. Taste it," she said. "Taste the poblano."

Antonio sliced his fork through the chile pepper. Queso blanco, softened when the pepper was grilled, oozed out of its seam. He scooped a piece of the poblano and cheese filling into his mouth and closed his eyes. I smiled at the show he made savoring the flavors.

We waited.

"Well? What do you think?"

He raised the palm of his hand to signal us to be quiet.

We waited.

He took another bite.

We waited.

Elena stamped her feet. "Antonio. You are playing."

When he spoke, it was not to us. Instead, he stood up on the bench, spread his arms and said to all within earshot. "¡Delicioso! I have never before had a chile like this one. The flavors delight the senses. The spice will tickle your tongue. Once you have tried one of these chiles, you will know the taste of heaven." Some stopped, looked at his plate, and placed an order.

Elena was so happy she glowed. Antonio had energized us both.

When he was about to leave, I thanked him for our full stand.

"Your chiles speak for themselves. They just need to be advertised."

"I still owe you eleven dollars plus interest, but I need more time and customers before I can repay you. We have been spending money on ingredients to try out new recipes."

"Has Elena told you about my filly?"

"No, not yet. Why?"

"Since her first race, we have had many good match races offered us. I have been careful to accept only the best challenges for her, and she has done very well. She is a strong contender. She is a favorite racer. Because of that, her odds are always set low by the gamblers. In her second race, I put a dollar on her nose for you. Each race afterward, I bet your winnings. Over several races, la Reina made you six more dollars. If we add in the cost of the rebozo you gave to my *novia*, my sweetheart, it totals more than you owe me."

"Antonio, the rebozo was a gift."

"An expensive one. Elena and I have talked about this. My filly will be a valuable broodmare. I can sell her colts for good prices. I have a good paying job. And I have luck at gambling. Elena and I will wed. I feel like a rich man." He lowered his voice, "You know how much I admire you, señorita Pérez. You owe me nothing. ¡Nada!" He winked at me, then walked to where Elena was serving and caressed her cheek with the back of his hand. He whispered to her something that raised her color, and sauntered off.

Antonio's generosity touched me—Elena's too. How could I accept so much? Elena should not have to pay for what was given as a gift. Besides, business was picking up, and if it continued to improve while we were on the plaza, I would be able to repay them, with interest. The rumor about a city hall worried me, though. I mulled the problem as I lay awake, waiting for sleep. I had nightmares about eviction. The thought was my first on awakening. I wished I could ask Peter. He would know what to do. We needed a plan.

"*Mamá, Papá, tenemos que hablar*. We need to talk."

They nodded. "*Sí, es cierto*. Yes, we do," Papá said. "The latest news is official. We have only a year left on Plaza de Armas."

The following Sunday evening, we sat down together to hot chocolate and fresh buttered tortillas. My older sisters with their husbands and children and my brothers with their wives and babies had left for their own homes. Papá asked señor and señora Hernández and Elena to join us. When everyone was seated around the table in the yard, I started:

"*¿Nos mudamos a otra plaza?* Should we move to another plaza?"

"Some of the chili vendors are talking about going to Alamo Plaza," Mamá said. "Would it be a good place for us, too?"

"There were lots of tourists there. But it adds distance," Papá answered. "So far as I know, there is no place there to store the stand. We would have to add the tables to the equipment and the food Caballo carts from the house."

"Plaza de Zacatecas is not so far away," señor Hernández said.

"Is there storage there?" I asked.

Papá shook his head. "I do not think so. And it does not have the centrality of Plaza de Armas."

"What about Washington Square?" señora Hernández asked.

"Same limitations," Papá said. "I am getting on in years. I do not have the strength of my youth. I cannot do heavy work for much longer."

Señor Hernández nodded.

"*¡Por supueso!* Of course," I called out. "Of course!"

Everyone looked at me.

"The question is not which plaza we should move to. The question is how do we avoid having to cart so many heavy things to where we serve? What if we did not cart our stand anywhere? What if we opened a *fonda*, a café, right here in our house, and use the yard for al fresco dining? Suppose we use your yard too?" I said to señor Hernández. "It adjoins ours. That would give us plenty of space."

Señora Hernández smiled. "¡Bueno!"

Mamá clapped her hands in approval.

Papá's sagging shoulders squared.

The ideas were coming to me quickly now, like water rushing through an open *acequia,* sluice.

"The front room where I now sleep could be our indoor dining area. If we move out the bed and chest, we could put tables in there."

"You can sleep with me," Elena offered.

I smiled at her and continued, "By doing all our cooking here, in time we can expand the menu. We have two cook fires, two sets of pots, two comals—and dos cooks. We could prepare many meals at the same time."

"We need more tables and chairs," Papá said.

"We have a year to do this," señor Hernández added. "We can find used tables and chairs and build others."

"Tablecloths. Napkins. Earthenware," señora Hernández said.

"We can save money from the profits each month to purchase furnishings," I added.

"Customers?" Elena asked. "How will our customers find us?"

"You will tell them, Elena," Mamá said.

"Have you seen the carte de visite that Sadie Thornhill gives out?"

Everyone at the table nodded.

"Good idea, Lupe," Papá said. "We can invest in some cartes de visite advertising our fonda with the address and directions from Military Plaza. We can hand them out to our patrons during our last months there."

With some effort, Papá slowly raised himself from the bench. We all turned toward him. I hoped he was not having second thoughts. When he finally spoke, it was an announcement. *"Debemos tener un nombre.* We must have a name. Something memorable. One that will make people think of us and no other chili stand on the plaza."

"What makes us distinctive?" señor Hernández asked.

"El Poblano," Elena and I blurted out as if one voice.

Everyone clapped.

"A year will pass quickly," Papá said. "We must prepare now."

CHAPTER 25

"Where? Where do you want this to go?" Antonio asked.

I looked at the diagram I had drawn of the front room of our house on the inside cover of my account book. Then I surveyed the empty room itself. Papá was moving one of the tables that he and señor Hernández had built with lumber purchased from our profits. We also had a couple of donated tables and matching chairs that señora Hernández got from families whose houses she cleaned.

"We can put one of the long tables along the side wall. The small ones will go in the center of the room, kitty-cornered here and there. Like this." I walked to each place, spreading my arms to show the desired position. "We have to leave space for Elena and me to walk completely around all the tables. The room is large enough for one rectangular and three square ones. We can serve as many as eighteen diners at once in here. More outdoors."

We had nice chairs for the used tables but not for the homemade ones. I would have preferred chairs, but Papá advised benches. They were less expensive, easier to make, and more versatile. They could be replaced with chairs later, he said. After all the furniture had been placed, Papá, Mamá, señor and señora Hernández, Elena, Antonio, and I stopped to assess the layout.

"We need cloths for the small tables," I thought out loud. "One red, then green, then blue on the square ones and red on the rectangular table. And we will wear white." I smiled. "The Mexican and American colors."

"What about napkins?" Elena asked. "The same colors as the tablecloths?"

"Sí. If we have as many customers each night as we have at the stand, we could use forty or fifty each night. We will have to wash every day. A dozen cost one and two bits. We should buy five dozen, and extra tablecloths, too."

"*¿Las luces?* Lights?" Papá asked. "The lanterns are too big for the tables. We could put the ones we use at the stand by the front door, two outside and two in this room. We will need to get more for the room and the yard. Candles—nice stout ones—can light each table, with several at the longer tables, in here and outside."

"Just imagine what it will look like, the cloth-draped tables in candlelight." I swept my arm through the space, over the bare tables. In my mind's eye, flickering candlelight illuminated brightly colored tablecloths and softly played across the faces of gregarious diners.

By far the most expensive purchase was the dresses for Elena and me. I wanted us both in white so we would stand out against the strong blue, green, and red table dressings. I had longed for one from the day I first saw young women in white dresses at San Pedro Springs Park. But after earthenware and flatware purchases were added to the budget, furnishings alone had almost depleted our reserves. The Bloomingdale and Sears and Roebuck catalogs showed many dresses I liked, but at prices we could not afford.

"You will be the hostess," Elena had said. "You could buy one of these dresses with less than what it would cost to dress both of us."

"No." I was adamant. "I want us dressed similarly, all in white, with vivid rebozos in contrast. We would be different, striking, appealing. I wanted to dress your mamá and mine in white too, but they have declined. Impractical, they say."

"It is not practical for us, either, Lupe. We cannot indulge in new dresses now. We will just have to do without for a while."

"*¡Espera!* Wait! In the summertime, San Pedro Park is awash in white. There must be many white dresses stored in trunks and wardrobes. Some women may be happy to get a little money to buy new for next summer."

Elena's eyes widened. "My mamá may be able to help. In the same way she found the tables."

Two weeks later, Elena rushed into our house. She was breathless. "Lupe, Mamá has a surprise."

"White dresses?"

Elena's curls bobbed with her vigorous nod. She was excited. "Can you come now?"

I dropped the chemise I was mending and followed her into the Hernández house.

Señora Hernández was waiting for us. She led us into her bedroom where two white dresses lay across the bed.

One dress had sleeves of lace, the same lace as its yoke, edged in scallops. Fullness in the bodice was gathered at the waist with a bow belt of the same fabric. The floor length skirt was finished with a scalloped hemline to match the yoke.

The other had a high-collared bodice trimmed with lace that formed a V from neck to waist. The long skirt's hemline was edged with a soft ruffle made from the same lace. A satin ribbon belt tied into a bow at the back.

"*Son hermosos*. They are beautiful, señora Hernández. Where did you get them?"

"Mrs. Frost knows a great many people," she answered. "When I told her that my daughter and her best friend were looking for white dresses, her first response was that the season was not right. When I told her why you wanted them, Lupe, she was impressed by your initiative. She agreed to ask her friends. When I went back to clean her house, she had these two waiting for me. They are from the wardrobes of young women like you. Take your pick."

"¿Cuánto? How much do the owners want?" I asked. "I have seen dresses like these in the Bloomindale catalogue. They must have cost twenty or thirty dollars each."

"Mrs. Frost said that if you can use the dresses, their owners are happy to give them to you. They plan to buy new for the coming summer. There is no cost. You could send Mrs. Frost a note of thanks."

"How generous—and helpful. I will write thank-you notes to each of the young women who donated their dresses and enclose them with the one I send to Mrs. Frost."

"I am sure that they will be pleased to receive them, Lupe."

I admired the fine-quality dresses. "Elena should have first choice."

Elena looked from me to her mother and back again. We nodded. She did not hesitate, picking the one with the scalloped lace yoke and hem. We tried on the dresses. Elena's fit her perfectly. Mine needed alteration.

Señora Hernández said she could let out a couple of seams and take a few tucks to fit it to me. We would be ready for opening night.

We chose the evening of Friday, the eleventh of January of '89, to debut El Poblano. Luck was with us. Temperatures all week had ranged from the midthirties to the low fifties, comfortable for the physical work of moving furniture, putting last minute touches on décor, and, most importantly, preparing the food. By sundown, a dry cool breeze would make for an invigorating walk to our house on Laredo Street from points east of San Pedro Creek.

Two ornate tin lanterns lighted our front doorway, where I stood in my white dress with the family's heirloom rebozo wrapped about my shoulders, its fringes swaying as I moved. Regulars at our stand on Military Plaza tentatively found their way into Laredito, a part of town some had not visited before. They smiled in recognition when they saw me. I showed them to tables and chatted briefly with each. Elena explained our menu and took their orders.

By half past eight, the fonda was lively with diners. By nine, it was packed, indoors and out. Some had come out of curiosity. Others for the specialty of the house, still reasonably priced. Some said they had come in support of us.

On each table was a small bowl of chile chips and our chile sauce for dipping. Diners munched on those while Elena and I took their orders to Mamá and señora Hernández at the cooking stations in the yard. They had divided the cooking chores between them and were preparing plates and tortillas rapidly. Papá handled the money. Señor Hernández walked among diners offering candies and cigarettes for sale.

I looked around the softly lighted room. Candlelight took on the colors of the tablecloths, just as I had imagined. Lantern light made the room warm, inviting, and romantic.

Antonio had gotten permission from Mr. Illg to leave the shop earlier that day. He had come by for last-minute setup, then had gone home to change into clean clothes. Now, he stood in the doorway. He was wearing a white shirt buttoned at the neck and finished with a bandana tie. His dark hair was neatly combed. He was clean-shaven. Playfully, I flicked the colorful fringes on the family's heirloom rebozo at him. But then he startled me when he began to clap his hands, long and loud. The place went silent as everyone looked in his direction.

"This is a wonderful fonda. Do you agree?"

The diners clapped loudly.

Antonio held up his hands for quiet. "But there is something missing that we all know is the source of the Pérez magic."

The diners looked at one another, unsure of Antonio's meaning.

"Lupe's stories," he shouted. "We must hear one of Lupe's stories, especially on this memorable night."

And then it came, feet stomping, hand clapping, whistles, and the call, "A story. Una historia, señorita."

Guests dining outdoors gathered at the entryway to the yard to see what all the commotion was about.

I held up my arms, the rebozo swaying as I did so, turned to my left, then to my right, to embrace all our guests. "Bueno. You will have one of my best. I will tell my tale in here, then do the same for our al fresco diners."

With my reassurance, some returned to their tables outdoors to continue their own conversations and wait for my tale. But others stayed, lining the walls to hear me.

"Tell the one about the girl cowhand," a man dining with a pretty woman called out.

"How about the meeting with Quanah Parker," an elderly man in a well-tailored jacket said.

Several cowboys at the long table were in animated conversation. One of them spoke for the group. "Our favorite is about horse racing with the Comanches."

"I will pick one for tonight. You will have to return on Monday night for another."

I looked back at Antonio. He was taking bets.

Señor Hernández still spent several hours a day on Military Plaza selling his candies, gathering news, and spreading word about El Poblano. He kept us informed about what was going on there. Vendors on Military Plaza were getting official eviction notices. They were told to vacate the plaza before construction on the city hall started. Regular diners were lamenting the move of chili stands away from the marketplace and entertainment hub that Military Plaza had been. "Where will we find you?" they asked of chili queens still there. Managers of hotels and tourist attractions had the same question. Some of the chili queens did not yet know where they would relocate. We were ahead of them all. Elena's father handed out our cards announcing El Poblano, identifying it as the Pérez fonda, with hours, location, and directions from Military Plaza. And so we had a steady flow of customers.

One day, señor Hernández told us that he had met a reporter from the *San Antonio Light* who was on the plaza to do an article about its transition from market place to the seat of city government. "*Se presentó como* Henry Ramsey. He introduced himself as Henry Ramsey," he told us. "He took one of our cards. Said that he might come by one day."

"That would be good for us," Elena said.

"*Es posible que escriba un artículo sobre El Poblano para el periódico.* He might do a story about El Poblano for the newspaper," señora Hernández said.

I did not say, but I doubted that a small Mexican café in the Laredito neighborhood would interest readers of the *San Antonio Light*.

Several weeks later, a tall, slender man I had not seen before arrived at our front door. El Poblano had been open for several hours, and I was just finishing my story about Miguel Martinez crossing the flooded Red River on horseback, naked. The stranger stood just inside the doorway, listening. His gaze was so intense, I felt self-conscious. I flounced my rebozo to signal an end to the story, draped it over my shoulders, and went to greet the newcomer.

He was pushing back an unruly lock of light brown hair when I looked up into brown eyes shaded by a squared brow. His face was long and lean. Not handsome. Pleasant. Open. His mouth was upturned in a broad smile. "Señorita Pérez?"

I nodded. "Welcome to El Poblano."

He showed me the card that had brought him. "A candy man on Military Plaza gave me this and told me a little about what you have done. I came to see how a chili stand was made into a café."

"We are flattered, Mr. . . ."

"Ramsey. Henry Ramsey."

"Mucho gusto, Mr. Ramsey. Would you like a table?"

He nodded and I showed him to one. Elena was quick to provide a place setting and rattled off the menu. He ordered our poblano especial.

"Try some of our chile chips while you wait for your meal," I suggested.

"I would like to talk with you."

"Gladly, as soon as I am free." I left him to enjoy the chips and Mamá's chile sauce while I greeted an arriving couple.

Elena had perfected her serving skills at our chili stand and in the fonda. She was graceful, efficient, and attentive to the customers. I knew that she would serve Mr. Ramsey with panache.

I watched him from the corner of my eye as I visited with other diners. When he was close to finishing his meal, I returned to his table to ask if there was anything else he might wish. "I can visit now," I said and sat opposite him.

He drew a sheaf of papers and a pencil out of his jacket pocket. "Is it all right if I take notes on what you say? I want to interview you for a newspaper story."

"Of course." His request was both exciting and troubling. *A newspaper story could be good for business*, I thought. *If it is positive. Newspaper reporters could be critical. Be careful.*

"I am told that you have poblanos for each night—all different."

"The poblano is our signature dish. We have spent many hours perfecting different combinations of ingredients to find the most flavorful, most interesting ones to put into our chiles. If you come back tomorrow, you can try another."

"Perhaps I will." He looked at me intently. "Señorita Pérez, why did you decide to open a café instead of moving your stand to another plaza?"

I told him as he rapidly made notes on his paper. That question was followed by others that revealed all that we had done to start our fonda. He filled the papers with neat and tightly drawn handwriting.

"It is about time for me to entertain my patrons with a story," I said. He rose as I did, then sat down again, ordered another coffee, and turned to listen.

I decided on a story that I had first told to Peter, the one about the prison breakout from the city jail on my favorite plaza. It was a uniquely San Antonio story that I thought a newspaper reporter would enjoy.

Henry Ramsey returned every night that week and regularly for several weeks thereafter. And every time he came, he asked me more questions about our foods, my stories, the songs, and even our rebozos. He would take notes as he did the first night, then fold the papers and stuff them into his jacket pocket. He became a regular diner, sampling every type of chile relleno we made in addition to our chips, chili, and enchiladas.

One night, he arrived with a newspaper under his arm. He opened it on the table and tapped his finger against a page. I brought the candle closer to see. Within the closely packed black print of a city news column I saw the title. I sat down and read further. Henry Ramsey's printed words touched my heart.

Chili Queen Opens Café on Laredo Street
With the impending construction of City Hall on Military Plaza, Miss Guadalupe Pérez and family have transformed their chili stand into a café. Resplendent with colorful tablecloths and glowing in the light of lamps and candles, El Poblano serves diners delectable chile chips with spicy chile sauce of distinctive flavor. Their signature stuffed poblano pepper changes its filling every night for a tasty surprise. The traditional diner can still order chili and frijoles or enchiladas smothered in chile sauce and topped with onion and cheese. The hungry patron will have his appetite satisfied and his thirst quenched with hot chocolate, coffee, or a thick and hearty cup of a sweetened chocolate and cornmeal mix called atole. Miss Pérez charms with stories and songs of the cattle drives of old and events in our city. Resident and tourist alike will have a complete evening's entertainment at 317 West Laredo Street. Look for the busiest house on the block. When you step inside, your senses will be rewarded with spicy aromas and the sight of pretty young women in white dresses and colorful Mexican shawls.

"This is the best advertising we could hope for," I told him. "Your meal is on the house tonight."

"This is just the beginning. If my editor agrees, I would like to run a series of articles in the paper about you, your chili stand, this fonda."

"I have something I would like to show you," I told him. "I will bring it to you."

I hurried into the adjoining room and lifted the lid on the chest where we stored our personal possessions. Carefully, I pulled the keepsake in its cloth wrapping from the very bottom of the trunk and rushed back to Mr. Ramsey's table. He rose to greet me.

"This," I told him, "marks the time my story started."

I placed my treasure on the table, carefully peeling back the wrapping.

He held it in both hands, his eyes scanning every detail. "Is that you?"

I nodded. "This is the photograph Mr. Hardesty took of me at our chili stand. That day, I had gone to the plaza with my father and brother to set up for the evening. When Mr. Hardesty gave me this print, he said, 'Señorita Pérez, I hope that this photograph will be memorable for you.' My first wonderings about how to improve business at our stand were forming when he captured my image. That night my explorations began. I had no idea where or how far they would take us—take me."

Chili Stands, Military Plaza, San Antonio, 1886. Courtesy of the Witte Museum, San Antonio, Texas.

Henry Ramsey studied the image, looked at me, then back at the photograph. When he spoke, his eyes were dancing. He was beaming.

"You have an inspiring story to tell, señorita Pérez. It needs to be told as a memoir, with your recipes, your historias, your songs. I want to help you tell it, the whole of it, from the beginning of your efforts to now—for people here and elsewhere to know, today and long after our lifetimes. Will you help me?"

And so this book came to be.

FURTHER ACKNOWLEDGMENTS
& notes for readers

The *stories* told by the chili queens in this novel were inspired by oral histories in *The Trail Drivers of Texas*, edited by J. Marvin Hunter and George W. Saunders, copyright obtained in 1924 by George W. Saunders and in 1925 by Lamar & Barton, agents, and published in 1985 by the University of Texas Press. The collection was reprinted in 1992 by the University of Texas Press with an added introduction and index. Stories about events in San Antonio were adapted from reports in 1880s issues of the *San Antonio Daily Express* and the *San Antonio Light*.

In Chapter 2, Lupe is intrigued by Martha Garcia's tale of the Ben Thompson and King Fisher shooting. That version of the story was taken from newspaper sources and G. R. Williamson's *Texas Pistoleers: The True Story of Ben Thompson and King Fisher*, first published in 2010 by The History Press, Charleston, SC.

Songs known to the chili queens were sung at home, on the trail, and on the border. The English language songs in this book appear in *Cowboy Songs and Other Frontier Ballads* by John A. Lomax and Alan Lomax, published by Collier-Macmillan Canada Ltd., the Macmillan Company, in 1938. The Spanish language songs appear in *A Texas-Mexican Cancionero: Folksongs of the Lower Border*, by Américo Paredes, published by The University of Illinois Press in 1976 and reprinted with permission by the University of Texas Press in 1994.

Recipes for Mexican food are based on foods served at chili stands that 1880s newspaper reporters described in their articles. Some are adapted from a handwritten Spanish cookbook, *Cocina Mexicana* [MS cookbook TX 715.M4 C6553 1880z] in the Rare Books Collection of the University of Texas at San Antonio Libraries Special Collections. All have been prepared and taste tested by my friends and me in my kitchen.

The value of *currency* from 1885 to 1888, the time frame of this story, is as follows: four cents were equivalent to the relative worth of a US dollar today, according to the Consumer Price Index (CPI). The CPI measures the cost of typical household purchases such as food, clothing, and transportation. One cent was equivalent to today's dollar using the Unskilled

Wage measure of the relative value of unskilled wages over time. Source: measuringworth.com.

The *Mexican cowhand* is known as a *vaquero*, the forerunner of the American cowboy. Many of the articles of clothing and equipment and the methods used by cowboys originated with the vaquero and continue to bear their Spanish names. Bandana, lasso, and lariat are just a few of many.

Charreadas are rodeos that were first held on haciendas in Mexico. They were brought to Texas by vaqueros and continue to this day. During these competitive events, vaqueros demonstrate their horsemanship and cattle ranching skills.

Marian L. Martinello has enjoyed a forty-year career as a public school teacher in New York and California and a university professor at the City University of New York (CUNY), the University of Florida, and the University of Texas at San Antonio (UTSA), receiving several teaching awards and earning distinction as a Minnie Stevens Piper Professor. She earned bachelor's and master's degrees at Queens College of CUNY and a doctorate from Columbia University's Teachers College. She holds the title of professor emeritus at the University of Texas at San Antonio and currently serves as president of the UTSA Retired Faculty Association. Her publications include studies of inquiry learning, interdisciplinary curriculum and teaching, and award-winning books on the history and cultures of Texas. She has previously published *The Search for Emma's Story* (1987), *The Search for Pedro's Story* (2006), and *The Search for a Chili Queen* (2009) with TCU Press. After moving to San Antonio in 1975 to become a founding faculty member at UTSA, she became intrigued with the rich local history and diverse cultures of South Texas, an interest that permeates her writing of nonfiction and fiction.